TORMENT

THE MANAGER

--- PULLING THREADS ---

Book Ten

SHERYLL O'BRIEN

This is a work of fiction. All characters in this book are the product of an overactive imagination. Any businesses, organizations, places, events, and incidents are used fictionally. Any resemblance to a real person, living or dead, is a tremendous coincidence.

ISBN 978-1-939351-29-6

WOODWIND PRESS

Printed in United States of America

Mom,

And your other threat,
"I don't care who you kill off,
but it better never be Fred!"

ACKNOWLEDGMENT

To my husband, Tim. Thank you for the time you spend in your office reading my books. I certainly appreciate your commitment to the series, but I really enjoy the peace and quiet. Love you, Mr. Wonderful.

A heartfelt thank you to my team:

Andria Flores ~ Editor extraordinaire.
Nancy Pendleton ~ Goddess of the publishing world.
Jessica Champion ~ Web designer and manager.
25 Hours Consulting
Daryl Bruinsma ~ Cover Design & Animation.

Testimonials

"One book will set the hook!" ~ Nancy Pendleton

"This avid reader predicts that Sheryll O'Brien will become your favorite author. She's mine." ~ Ruth S. Bodreau

"The characters draw you in immediately. You will worry, laugh, hope, and love right along with them." ~ Donna Eaton

"There is nothing sweeter than a Sunday morning coffee, a blanket, overcast skies, and a *Pulling Threads* novel." ~ Andria Flores

"Everything you'd want in a good book. Humor, romance, suspense and great characters! It even takes place by the ocean! Loved it." ~ Helena Green

"I could write a book about the wonderfulness of it all." ~ Faith Lavallee

"Hunks, humor, and heartache! What more could you ask for?" ~ Marjorie McCarthy

"*Bullet Bungalow* is a page turning family saga and then *Netti Barn* and *Cutters Cove* come along and add a whole lot of trauma to the drama." ~ Jessica O'Brien

"The most promising new author I've encountered in my publishing career!" ~ Jim P. - Woodwind Press

--- Pulling Threads ---

Bullet Bungalow
Netti Barn
Cutters Cove
They Run
They Hide
They Choose

PENOBSCOT BAY
A Rocco Fiancetti Incorporated Investigation

Reasons
Rescues
Resolutions
Torment

Coming soon…

Tango
Tests
Resolve
Revenge
Rebound

--- Twisted Threads ---

Coming soon…

Her Scream
Stay Safe

Tower of Power

Abigail Forrester is pissed. She has been in a raging mood since August 1st. That's the day Malcolm Price fired her from his mayoral campaign. For more than a month now, his parting words have banged a torturous beat in her head…

"Some things happened last night of which you are unaware, Abigail. I believe they will affect your plans. Micky Strong was arrested and is being held on charges in the murder of Sage Finley. So the dirt you've been trying to dig up on me, to force me from this race, is gone. Your leverage is gone." **Malcolm paused a minute before continuing.** "I will be filing Intent papers, and I will be running for mayor. I will also be making a statement on August 5th – the anniversary of the murder of Sage Finley, a beautiful young woman, whom I loved once upon a time. I will be telling our story and answering for my shortcomings. You are fired. You will not be saying a single word about Sage between now and my statement. If you do, I will put every penny I have into finding out why you want me out of Pennsylvania politics."

Abigail looked as though she was about to speak.

Malcolm spoke instead, "Get out."

The seething woman picks up a wooden block from her desk, turns it over and reads the written name on the bottom. "Malcolm Price," she hisses as she moves the block from one hand to the other and back again. "**You** were supposed to be my newest block, Mr. Price, an important part of my Tower of Power – not the most important playing piece, but." The woman admires the impressively tall tower of wooden blocks set in the center of her desk. She takes a minute to remind herself of the investment she's made in its construction. "I have painstakingly plotted and planned, maneuvered and manipulated, played and laid most every man who is represented by a block on that tower." She lifts one of the rectangular pieces and reads the etched name on the bottom, "Benton Brettenvue." Abigail laughs, then sneers, "You are terrible in so many ways, Benton, particularly between the sheets, but you've been useful in helping me inch toward my ultimate goal – though you almost fucked me royally with that whole Antonio Alvarez debacle..."

"I don't like coming here, Benton."

"Don't worry, Celia is out of town."

"I don't give a rat's ass about your wife. It's the fucking FBI knocking on your door **and** my door that freaks me out. Next time you want to introduce me to some international crime lord, don't."

Benton scoffed, "There isn't going to be a next time. Antonio Alvarez is behind bars. Cappa Escobar is dead. The Realm is disbanded. And Dominique is serving a life-sentence. The FBI hasn't been able to prove my involvement with any of the shit that's gone down. I am free and clear and so are you."

"What about Roland Gaffney?"

"What about him?" **Benton stopped his roaming and stared at Abigail.**

She stared back. "The former Director of FICA is sitting in a Federal prison on charges of treason because of his association with The Realm. I'm sure he's expecting help from someone—that means that there **is** someone—someone powerful enough to make sure Gaffney doesn't sing."

"Don't know. Don't want to know, Abigail."

"Don't bother with the bullshit, Benton. You know you're up to your ass in **it** and **it** has everything to do with The Realm."

Abigail places Benton's block back onto the tower, "You almost dragged my ass into that fucking shit show. Won't happen again. The next time the Feds come knocking on my door, they'll be getting the goods on you, Benton Brettenvue." She goes back to the other block in her hand, "Malcolm Price," she runs her fingers over the blonde woodgrain, "You may have put up a roadblock, you may have forced me to take an alternate route, but you will not keep me from reaching my destination, Mr. Price."

Abigail handles the block a bit more then places it into a desk drawer. She wants to slam that drawer closed, but rather, she inches it shut. "No sense in bringing down the whole damned tower because Malcolm Price bested me. This time."

From a television located one floor below her office, there comes a thunderous roar. A studio audience is showing its unrestrained enthusiasm when they hear that Malcolm Price has arrived at WNEP for an interview on *Sunday PA*. Abigail drains the last few sips of a way-too-early Kahlua sombrero and indulges in one more mental review of that August morning, the one that has temporarily detoured her course…

Malcolm Price had his wife and mother by his side as he filed his Intent papers at the Borough Office and on stage at the announcement at Hufnagle Park. The crowd of more than two thousand went wild when 77 introduced his new wife and announced the impending birth of 78.

The only person in the crowd not celebrating was Abigail Forrester. She made eye contact with the mayoral candidate and waited for his attention to be pulled away before issuing a quiet threat. "I may not have Sage Finley to use against you, but there's something in your past that will bring you to your knees." Abigail takes one more surveying look at the stage.

"The mother. Let's take a peek-see into her past."

Torment

Out for blood.

Mayoral candidate, Malcolm Price, enters WNEP for his fifth sit down interview since Micky Strong was taken into custody for the murder of Sage Finley in 2007. In the month since Malcolm kicked off his campaign, he has answered every conceivable question about his relationship with Sage…

"Did you meet Sage Finley at a Spurs meet and greet? … Did you know she was at the playoff game that night as a paid escort? … Did you steal her from her regular customer, Micky Strong? … Did Finley become your personal working girl? … Did you ever pay for her services? … Did you lie to investigators? … Did you intentionally obstruct a murder investigation? … Is Sage Finely buried at your ranch in Texas? … Did you love Sage Finley? … Did your wife know about your relationship with the working girl? … Do you think this will affect your election? … Should the people of Lewisburg trust you with their borough when you were less than truthful with the police? … Isn't your best friend Captain Damian 'Jet' Johnson? … How does he feel about your hindering an investigation?"

Malcolm expects today's interview will be much of the same—it is anything but.

"Good morning, Lewisburg, this is Jane Devereaux, host of *Sunday PA* and with us in the studio is Malcolm Price. Most of you know our mayoral candidate as 77, two-time NBA Champion with the San Antonio Spurs. For the next couple of months, you will know him as the front runner in the mayoral special election, and if the polls are correct you will be calling him Mr. Mayor on November 5th."

Chants of "77" fill the studio. Someone from the back answers with the former player's call back, **"Is In The House!"** The audience goes wild.

"Well, that's quite the welcome from your fans. Let me extend my personal welcome to *Sunday PA*, Mr. Price."

"Thank you Jane, and call me Malcolm."

The audience starts their second round of "77" calls and throws in a robust round of applause and foot stomping.

"Okay. Okay. Let's settle down and give Malcolm a chance to speak. It's been a month since you announced your run for mayor of Lewisburg. Since then, most of the media's focus has been on you and Sage Finley. There really hasn't been much attention paid to the other woman in your life—the one who may negatively affect your campaign. So tell me what you think about the race now that Abigail Forrester has thrown back in as campaign manager for your opponent, Topher Griffin?"

Malcolm smiles wide, "I think Topher helped lower the unemployment rate in the Commonwealth of Pennsylvania by hiring Ms. Forrester. That's a good thing."

Jane throws a chuckle and an approving nod his way, "The rumor is that Abigail Forrester is out for blood—your blood—for firing her from your campaign. Any comment?"

The very relaxed Malcolm gently shakes his head, "My comment is that some campaigns want to turn politics into a blood sport. The Malcolm Price Campaign for Mayor will only draw blood if there's a battle on behalf of the good people of Lewisburg. Personal vendettas have no place in this race."

Another robust round of applause fills the studio.

"So your campaign is taking the high road," Jane pushes.

Malcolm smiles wide, "That's the best road to take Jane, and with the help of the great people of Lewisburg, we hope to take the high road directly to the Borough Office." Malcolm leans in and addresses his host. "Jane, you and I can spend our time together rehashing my association with Ms. Finley, or you can allow me something that no other interviewer has offered."

"And that is?"

"An opportunity to talk about my plans for the people of Lewisburg. I do have a few ideas and workable plans for our little borough," he smiles w.i.d.e.

She does too, then she nods. "Let's set ourselves apart from the rest, Mr. Price."

Malcolm gets up and kicks it Town Hall style. He addresses the audience—his constituents. "The central focus of my work as mayor is twofold: enhancing our educational system and ensuring responsible stewardship of our environment. As you know, Lewisburg has a lot to be proud of when it comes to its public schools and institutions of higher learning. There is little need for change there; our educators and administrators are doing commendable work. But we all know they could use help, and not just from members of the educational community, but from everyone in Lewisburg. Our kids go to school to learn, so let's teach them what it means to be part of a community."

Malcolm waits through a bit of enthusiasm from the audience.

"My administration will focus on bridging the gap between getting good grades and what those grades can mean to the student, to his or her family, and to their community. To achieve that, I will call upon every business in the borough of Lewisburg to partner with a particular school. There will be a financial ask, but more importantly there will be an expectation that representatives of their organizations be present inside the classrooms, at assemblies, at the ballgames, and at celebrations. An ask that everyone helps inspire our kids to find the bridge between getting good grades and turning those grades into achievable actions."

"A mentorship…" someone calls out from the audience.

"A partnership. I want everyone to have skin in the game, the student, their family members, the grocer on their corner, the Market Street merchant, as well as the CEOs of our biggest employers." Malcolm makes his way back to his seat and addresses his host, "I have spent the last month listening to members of the Press and folks on the street talking a whole lot about me."

The audience throws in a laugh.

He ignores it. "As it relates to my entering politics, I've heard things like, 77 is running for mayor, two-time NBA Champ wants to be mayor, he sure played that game."

"And …" Jane wants more from him.

"And all of that is true. I played professional basketball and had my fair share of success. In all that's been said and written about my adult life, I've heard and seen nearly nothing about the things that helped me get to where I am today. I came up in the Lewisburg public school system and studied at Bucknell University. Those are the two things that allowed me to have every bit of my success. That is the message I will be bringing when I spend time with Lewisburg students. Now let's talk about the environment."

The audience listens with rapt attention, then throws thunderous support for their candidate of choice, The Malcolm Price.

After spending nearly an hour shaking hands with audience members, Malcolm heads backstage to the green room. He embraces his campaign manager and wife, Gretchen Mitchell.

"Nice job," she says before kissing her man. "I love that your host recognized the golden opportunity you presented, and that she took it. Even though you are ahead in the polls, we don't want people voting for you because of your celebrity status, we want them to know that you have substantive thoughts and plans."

He pulls her to him, "Yes, ma'am."

She gives him a quick peck, then hones in, "You know, Malcolm, Jane Devereaux is one of the most informed reporters in the business. If she went on record, on **her** show, that Abigail is out for blood—then Abigail is out for blood. That push by Jane begs the question: What weapon is Abigail going to use to draw that blood now that she doesn't have Sage Finley?"

The candidate doesn't answer the question—
although he could.

The bloodhound.

Abigail is setting her mind on dragging her ass into the campaign office of Christopher 'Topher' Griffin having made a miserable drive in from Philly. She sighs relief when she sees that Topher's car isn't parked on the lot. "Insufferable twit," she disparages, "but a necessary means to an end."

The candidate for mayor, who is **way down** in the polls, likes to call the minimally staffed, 1,000 square foot campaign office, the "War Room," though Abigail is reasonably sure he knows there won't be a single skirmish between the two candidates—let alone an actual war being waged. She grouses the reality of the situation, "Malcolm Price is going to win the election handedly unless I find something that will make him unelectable. I **need** Price out and Griffin in. My plans, the ones I've been working on forever, will be realized only if Griffin is mayor of Lewisburg and then governor of Pennsylvania. No fucking b-baller is going to fuck with my plans."

The fired-up redhead slams her car door and storms the frontlines. She spends a few minutes with the staff then locks herself in her office. All eyes are upon her as she paces her fishbowl space contemplating which weapon she can use against her target. "There's **nothing** on the Charlize Theron lookalike. The UPenn and Harvard Law graduate spent every waking minute in college with her nose pressed in textbooks or her ass running track and field competitions. There isn't a scintilla of gossip about her with some other guy. Gretchen Mitchell is one boring bleach blonde." Abigail sits down then immediately pushes away from her desk and stands in front of a window that looks out over the backend of Hufnagle Park, the place Malcolm Price chose for his announcement…

Abigail took a seat opposite her new boss and began outlining her schedule and plans. "For the next two weeks, I'll be devoting my time to the August 1st announcement. I have a list of venues that we should discuss."

"Hufnagle Park," Malcolm said.

"For what?"

"The announcement. It will be made at Hufnagle Park."

Abigail slumped a bit in her seat. "You can't be serious."

"Abigail, I am always serious and rarely flexible. I will seek your expertise when I need it. Assess whether you can work within those confines. Now, if you will excuse me, I have another meeting." Malcolm stood and waited for Abigail to follow his lead.

Her face flushes at the memory—her hands clench with anger. She drops back onto her desk chair and keystrokes a series of queries into a search engine, then writes the information into a notebook. Some of what she wants to know is readily available. Some, not so much.

Malcolm Price

Mother: Bertha King Price
Residence: Lewisburg, Pennsylvania
DOB: 1965
Place of birth: Savannah, Georgia
Family history: none listed
Father: Unknown

"I need Penny Meehan to dig in this pile of dirt." Abigail stops her strategizing at the sound of a knock on her office door. She waves in the candidate, barely suppressing a groan, "You're in early, Topher."

He enters and shuts the door behind him. "I'm having some residuals with you, Abigail. I didn't appreciate your dumping me for Price, even if you did it so you could maneuver behind the scenes. We both know you'd cut off my balls if something better came along." Topher eyes her good before continuing, "I know you have plans for me once I get elected mayor and governor, but it's best that you remember that I have goals of my own. Don't think for a single moment that I'm like soon-to-be-former Mayor Jack Cane. You won't get blackmail shit on me," he pauses, "Yes, Abigail, even I managed to put two and two together on his sudden departure from the political scene. This is fair warning, I will bark to the world what your intentions are, and I will bite you in the ass if you try to undercut my goals."

The fiery redhead tempers her internal burn and measures her words. "I know you aren't like Jack. I forced him out of office because he was never going to turn Pennsylvania coal country into Pennsylvania fracking country. He's too connected to the William Penn plot of land he lives on to ever agree to rape and pillage his homestead. I should have known fracking in the Commonwealth would be a tough sell with him, besides once he was in office it became clear that he's incapable of getting to the next level. I can put you in as mayor and as governor, Topher. You have made a name for yourself on the fracking issue—for good or for bad. If I get you into the governor's seat, you and I get to do our thing with fracking—I get to do *everything* else. That's the agreement. Are you still in?"

"Get me elected," Topher demands.

Abigail points to her computer, "That's what I was working on when you came in."

The candidate turns to leave, "Then, by all means, get back to work."

Criminal memories.

Gretchen Mitchell asks Researcher Randy, a hipster dude, cyber specialist who's working on Malcolm's campaign, to join her in her office. "Close the door, please."

Randy swings it shut and locks it behind him, "Can't be too careful around here," he says with a knowing grin. The Kid, as Malcolm refers to him, is making note of the back-to-back invasions into the adjoining penthouse apartment by individuals who meant great harm to Gretchen…

At 2:30 AM the team received a text.
Escobar coming in.

Cappa Escobar, paid assassin of Antonio Alvarez, closed the door behind him. He inched to the stairs, leaned against a railing and looked upward. He climbed to the first landing, leaned against the railing and looked upward. He paused, he listened, he reviewed his plan, "Get in, get Price, get the puta, get the fuck out."

Malcolm and Fred pocketed their cell phones after reading the text. "Escobar is here," Malcolm said as he pulled Gretchen to her feet. He kissed the top of her head, "Go."

RFI Detective Fred Serpico and Gretchen Mitchell entered the elevator. When the door closed behind them, the RFI operative locked the elevator down. He reminded Gretchen, "Escobar isn't expecting the fire power we've got assembled, and since he likes to work alone, he's probably going to be alone. If that's the case, he won't make it as far as the living room." Fred stepped in front of Gretchen to pull her full attention. "I want you to listen to me. If the living room is breached, this elevator goes to the garage and you and I get out of 275. Do you understand?"

"But Malcolm is positioned in the living room."

"No buts, Gretchen."

The rest of the team got in place.

FBI Agent Patterson moved to his position outside the alley door.

Captain Johnson and a Lewisburg PD officer waited behind the sixth floor access hallway door.

RFI Detective, Manuel Xavier, tucked into a corner just inside the entranceway to the penthouse.

Malcolm pressed against a far wall in the living room opposite the elevator.

Escobar continued his climb and his routine. At each landing, he leaned against the railing, took a look upward, a pause, a listen, a review of his plan. "Get in, get Price, get the puta, get the fuck out." At the fifth floor landing he froze. He closed his eyes, listened, assessed. "Muffled sounds ... a theme song ... a television show." He pulled a breath and moved to the next floor—the sixth floor. He stopped at the landing, leaned against the railing, took a look upward, *and* a look downward. He started up the stairs, then abruptly stopped. A push of concern hit deep— a chill ran his spine—he pushed back against the nudge of doubt. "Alvarez wants this done. Kill the lawyer, send a message to the Brettenvues—each one of them! No one defies Alvarez—not even me." He reviews his plan again, "Get in, get Price, get the puta, get the fuck out." Escobar settled on the eighth floor landing. He waited a second before turning the knob. The contract killer entered the penthouse and realized he was in a trap a fraction—of a fraction—of a second before Manuel Xavier sprung it.

"Drop your weapon, Cappa, you're surrounded."

"Manuel Xavier," Cappa snarled at the sound of the former FBI agent's voice. "Mr. Alvarez will be pleased to know that you die tonight along with the puta." Escobar swung his arm toward Manuel, both men fired.

~

Micky Strong, former San Antonio PI and murder suspect, was in Malcolm Price's orbit, and he was flush with purpose. He leisurely walked through Hufnagle Park, found a bench that gave him a perfect view of 275 Market Street, placed a plastic bag onto the bench and patted the contents inside. "A ham and swiss on Rye, a can of soda, and a 13-inch box that holds a brand new 12-inch blade. What more could a man want? A gun," he answers with a pat at the waistband of his jeans. "Yup, I'm good to go."

Micky grabbed his bag and sprinted across the street when the underground parking garage door lifted. He walked a few steps away from the brick building when a black Land Rover pulled out. The killer of Sage Finley, the hopeful killer of Gretchen Mitchell, turned in time to get his first glimpse of 77 and his platinum blonde woman. As they headed down Market Street, he sprinted under the garage door before it closed tight. Several hours later, the Land Rover returned, and within minutes Mr. and Mrs. Price had parked and keyed in an access code to the privacy elevator. Micky had what he needed. He waited a few minutes then keyed in the code, "The elevator comes back empty, or the end game takes place in the garage." The elevator came back empty. Micky hopped inside, shut the door behind him, took a seat, and waited. "Next time you call for your steel box, you'll get the surprise of a lifetime, Mr. Malcolm Price."

The husband and wife were flat on their backs, on their bed, holding hands. They'd been alternating between staring at the darkened ceiling, and watching the minutes tick away on the digital clock. Malcolm's cell vibrated shortly after midnight startling Gretchen who quickly covered her rapidly beating heart with her trembling hand.

"It's Randy," Malcolm whispered to his wife, "What?" he whispered to The Kid.

"I hear noises coming from the staircase, maybe from the landing between the apartment and the campaign office. I think we have company."

Malcolm and Gretchen were on their feet and moving, "Captain Johnson was putting officers around the building, and in the alley. Maybe they moved inside. Stay on the phone, and do not leave the campaign office," Malcolm directed The Kid. The man on the move tucked one of his handguns into the waistband of his jeans, took the other in his hand. He motioned for Gretchen to follow him to the elevator and banged the call button, "Did you bring your cell?"

"Yes."

"When you get in, call Damian and ask if his men moved inside."

The elevator announced its arrival at the penthouse with a ping. Malcolm kissed Gretchen's head, "Get in and lock it down."

As the door began sliding open, Gretchen yelped in surprise, and grabbed hold of Malcolm's arm. He swung her as far behind his back as possible, "Micky," he growled at the man stepping off the elevator.

Both men raised and pointed handguns— Micky's was pointed at Gretchen. The glint of a butcher's knife in his other hand caught the terrified woman's eye.

"That's for you, honey," Micky snarled.

The woman survivor of those two attempts on her life sighs and reminds Randy, "The hitman is currently residing six-feet under, and the punisher resides in a Texas prison. I think it's safe to unlock my office door."

"Hard pass, Mrs. Mayor. We can't be too careful around here."

"Careful about what?" Malcolm asks.

Randy spins toward the imposing 6'5" man who seemingly appeared from thin air, "You're better at that appearing from nowhere thing than Batman. And by the way, that door was locked—produce the keys, or I'm telling everyone that you *are* Batman."

Malcolm points to a chair, "Sit. We were put on notice the other day by Jane Devereaux at WNEP that Abigail Forrester is out for blood. She wants mine, but she will accept a pint from anyone associated with me. Gretchen, what's our plan?"

"I was just about to formulate a research project with Randy. Do you want in?"

"Nope. I have a few things to deal with, then I'm heading for a shower."

"Meet you there," Gretchen winks.

Randy rolls his eyes, "The water bill for 275 must be astronomical. Think about that when you're crafting your environmental policy."

"Two people, one shower, less water—environmental policy done," Malcolm laughs as he leaves The Kid who he's come to think of as a younger brother—a younger, weirder brother.

Researcher Randy is 6' tall, has windblown surfer blonde locks, and a cared for scruff on his youthful face. He wears skinny jeans, plaid shirts, wool caps and Vans. He has mad computer and research skills and tends to move and shake outside the mainstream. The most important thing about Researcher Randy is that he has become one of Gretchen and Malcolm's most trusted cohorts.

She gets up from her desk, shuts the door behind Malcolm, and leans against it, "Randy, I know you're technically my husband's employee for the next few months, but the work I'm going to ask you to do needs to be kept between you and me."

"No can do, Mrs. Fill-In-The-Blank. We are not diving deep on 77. He already put us on notice about that."

"Not on Malcolm, well not technically," Gretchen smiles.

"Don't lawyer me, Miss Mitchell, or is it Mrs. Mitchell or is it Mrs. Mitchell-Price, or is it Mrs. Adjacent? Sure would have been easier if you took 77's last name when he hitched you to his wagon."

Gretchen chuckles, "It's Ms. Mitchell, although I'm rather fond of Mrs. Adjacent." Gretchen waits a minute then doubles down on the researcher, "Seriously, Randy, we need to try to find out what Abigail Forrester is up to. The first thing we need to know is where Malcolm might be vulnerable because that's where Abigail is headed. His first vulnerability was Sage, but she's at peace now. His next vulnerability is me, but I don't have any issues that could negatively affect him. So his last vulnerability is a two-part issue—his mother and his father."

"You want me to dive deep into Mama Girl and Mystery Dad?"

"I don't want you to, but I think that's on Abigail's agenda. There's a question already out there, and it's a big one—who is Malcolm's father? Then there are a whole lot of questions about Mama Girl—like why she left Savannah as a pregnant teen, and what she did to survive when she arrived in Lewisburg."

"Valid questions, Mrs. Adjacent, but if Mystery Dad is still a mystery, and Mama Girl hasn't shared her business, there's a reason." He pauses. He ponders. He continues. "I don't share the frizzy redhead's desire to know the answers, but I sure as hell don't want her to have the upper hand." Randy shakes his head for a minute before buying in. "When you're looking for me, I'll be in the reluctant corner diving deep into things that are none of my business."

I felt the baby move.

Mrs. Adjacent enters the adjoining penthouse apartment in search of her husband. She needn't look far—he is in his usual pose, back leaning against a wall with his long legs stretched out and crossed at the ankles. The wall upon which her man is currently leaning is the one just this side of the master bedroom.

Malcolm looks up from his cell when she enters the room. At four months pregnant his wife is sporting a perfectly round baby bump, and her boobs are a bit fuller—other than that, she is the woman who first caught and held his eye. Malcolm pushes off the wall when Gretchen gets near and pulls her against him. His erection evident against her belly.

"Been fantasizing about me again, Malcolm," she purrs.

"Get in the shower, Woman," he growls.

Gretchen scurries down the hallway and through the master bedroom losing pieces of clothing along the way. He follows suit. The near-naked man reaches past his woman to turn on the shower, his hand grazes one of her erect nipples, hers grazes his jutting wood.

She moans.

He groans.

He places his hand to their baby bump and she jumps back.

"Gretchen?" he reacts at her sudden movement, "the baby?"

She turns astonished eyes to him, "I felt the baby move. Oh, Malcolm, I felt 78."

He places his hopeful hand to her bump. She places her hand on top of his, "You won't feel it yet. I'm surprised I even felt it. It was so fleeting, like a tiny butterfly stretching its wings." She wraps her arms around her man and pulls her legs up and around his waist.

He walks them into the shower and slides her down until her feet find floor. He presses her against the wall and begins playfully arousing her with kisses here and touches there. His fingers find her willing and accepting. He brings her to a breath of release then enters her as her orgasm tightens around him. His release is immediate and powerful.

I need dirt on Malcolm Price.

Abigail Forrester waits on the line for Penny Meehan, a former tabloid reporter who somehow landed a gig at *Liberty Rings*, a century-old Central Pennsylvania newspaper.

Penny is s.l.o.w. in answering the phone. She is still miffed at Abigail for dragging her into the debacle regarding Sage Finley. Truth be told, the reporter is madder at herself for getting pulled away from the legitimate side of news. She takes a minute to scold herself, before answering the call, "You should have trusted your instincts — but Abigail made a compelling case..."

"You get the information on the basketball player and the call girl, and we make a 50/50 split. I use the smut to put an end to Malcolm Price's political aspirations, and you get to write a legitimate news story about a b-baller from Pennsylvania who settled in Texas and somehow convinced the whole damned state to cover-up his thing with Sage Finley. The piece could show how and why the people in Bastrop County extended loyalty to Price. Did they simply not care about his relationship with a hooker and his involvement in how she ended up dead – solely because he was 77? Or is there more to this story – maybe there were payoffs, threats and intimidation, or some felonious quid pro quo with some official? Penny, your ability to flush out the salacious combined with your legitimate journalistic chops makes this piece perfect for you. Do yourself a favor and stick your nose in – find out if there is more dirt swept under his rug – and then pull that rug out from under The Malcolm Price."

It was Malcolm Price who pulled the rug out from under them. The resilient Abigail Forrester landed a job with the Topher Griffin campaign, and Penny Meehan landed on her ass—**after** it was chewed out by a very angry editor. Penny put her 'nose for smut' to the grindstone and hasn't taken a call from Abigail since that debacle. Against her better judgment the reporter takes this call.

"What do you want, Abigail?"

"I need your investigative reporter chops."

"For what?"

"I need dirt on Malcolm Price."

"Been there—done that—and got a professional ass-reaming for my efforts. Besides, what makes you think there's more dirt on Price?"

"He's a man. Men have dirt. In this case, I think his mother has dirt, too," Abigail floats her balloon.

"What kind of dirt,"

Abigail smiles – she has Penny hooked, so she reels her in. "The name of Malcolm Price's father, for starters. The NBA legend known as 77, was the most written and talked about professional athlete for ten years, he's a two-time NBA Champion, he's running for political office, and NO ONE knows who his father is. Hell, Price probably doesn't even know who his father is. Why is that Penny?" Silence from the reporter's end makes the redhead think she may have disconnected from the call – she didn't.

"I'm in, but if you end up burning me, I'll be doing an article on you, Abigail, one that will ruin your career." Penny hangs up.

Abigail tosses her cell onto her living room couch, pours and drains a shot of Café Patron, before sitting on the stairs that lead to the second floor of her condo. She is waiting for an unwelcome guest – and reminding herself how she got to where she is today...

The high school student rolled her eyes when the guidance counselor called her name and waited for her to enter the tiny office, "Sit down Abigail," the do-nothing, paper-pusher said as she pretended to read Abigail's file, "You are an excellent student. Let's make a plan for what comes next."

"I've already made my plan for what comes next. I graduate in May, go to Blakesville College, get straight A's, get accepted into the Honors Program, get straight A's, get accepted into the internship program, and get the fuck out of Scranton," she said as she sauntered out of the office—the guidance counselor's words trailing after her, "You can take the girl out of Scranton, but …"

"…you can't make her come back again. Ever!" Abigail finished the sentence her own way.

~

"Blakesville is the best," Abigail's new roommate squealed as she unpacked her things. "It turns out well-educated, self-assured, competitive women" she continued, enthusiastically.

Abigail laughed. "Those are the highlighted promises on the College's brochures, but everyone knows that Blakesville girls are taught how to use what they have, to get what they want," Abigail took pleasure in the whole clutching of pearls response from her genteel roomie, then pushed in a bit more. "I know what I have – it's called a pussy – and I'm ready to use it. Senior year is going to be the best." Over the next many months, the redhead researched and readied herself for Plan Pussy having set her sights on Turner Rodgers, a forty-something, two-term Republican Congressman who had an internship opening in his DC office and a few problems keeping his dick in his pants.

Within weeks of her arrival in DC, Abigail was the Congressman's sexual release at the office. "Abigail, my piece of tail, lock the door behind you," Turner directed. Abigail locked it, leaned back against it, and unfastened the clip holding back her frizzy shoulder-length hair. She shook it free while she began unbuttoning her top.

"Leave your shirt on. This get-together isn't about pleasing you." Turner stood, unzipped his pants, and pulled his erection free. "Suck it."

Abigail crossed the room, applying a generous swipe of lip balm along the way, and got onto her knees. While in his office, the college intern spent most of her time face-down on the penis of the Republican Congressman. While out front, she spent most of her time elbow-deep in his personal files. That was where she learned that Turner Rodger's aspirations were high, and his sperm count was low – way too low to have fathered children with his wife. When Abigail Forrester turned the tables on Congressman Rodgers, she learned how far he would go to keep his wife's infidelity and his children's paternity a secret.

Tower of Power — construction underway.

Block number one.

Abigail extended her time in DC beyond her internship by attending Georgetown University courtesy of the generous, "Don't Tell Anyone I'm Sterile" scholarship fund of Turner Rodgers. She studied political science and government policy at GU by day and learned salacious secrets on the Hill by night.

Block number two.

Democratic Senator Eugene Jackson of Rhode Island, liked to rub his down-low boys across the ass of down-low boys barely out of their teens.

Block number three.

Republican Senator Leland Grayson of South Carolina, looked very fetching in corsets and garter belts and preferred leather whips over satin sashes.

Block number four.

Republican Senator Jeff Landers of Tennessee liked his hats pointy, his sheets white, and his country whiter.

Block number five.

Appellate Court Judge, Robert Cantor, hid the tracks of his addiction inside the full sleeves of his black robe.

Block number six.

DC Metropolitan Police Detective, Mason Trellis, brought home a lust for blood from his days in Special Forces.

By the time Abigail Forrester left the Nation's capital, she had salacious details about

Jackson, Grayson, Landers, Cantor, Trellis and a dozen others. She held onto the knowledge, etched their blocks, and set a solid foundation for her Tower of Power.

Abigail pulls herself from her thoughts and to the reason she is perched upon her stairs. Benton Brettenvue is stopping by for a shagging. She harrumphs, "There'll be no more shagging." Ever since the arrest and incarceration of his daughter, Dominique, and the FBI investigation of The Brettenvue Group, the CEO has become a liability—a drunken liability at that. The Group has gone from the top-rated lobbying firm in PA, to being on the precipice of collapse. Further, his performance in the sack has gone from tolerable to detestable. "It ends tonight," she reminds herself and prepares herself.

The woman-in-wait surprises the drunkard when he opens the front door. "You're late," she hisses from the stairs.

"You're a shrew," he slurs.

Abigail gets up, pushes past him, and walks to the middle of the living room. She extends her hand, palm up, "Give me my keys, we're through."

Benton bellows, "We're through when I say we're through. You'd better tread lightly, Abigail. I know where your bones are buried," he pauses, not for effect, but because he's blind drunk, "It's best you don't test my loyalties—because there are none."

Abigail laughs, "You can run your mouth about me for the next ten years and not inflict as much damage as I can with a single name — Antonio Alvarez."

Benton stumbles as he moves toward her, rights himself in time to deliver a slap across her face. She ducks a second swing of his hand, and knees him in the balls, "Get the fuck out, Benton!" The pissed redhead leaves the heaving man on the floor and climbs the first few stairs, "I'm calling the police in one minute, so get the fuck out of my house."

Benton stumbles to his car – one hand holding his throbbing balls, the other struggling to open the door. He falls in – does a bit of drunk-laughing when he notices Abigail's keys still on his keyring, "They'll come in handy one day, you bitch." He starts his car, reaches onto the passenger seat, and grabs one of several open whiskey bottles that litter the interior of his brand-new BMW Alpina. He unscrews the top of a bottle and puts it to his lips; he is tilting his head back to pull a swig when he sees the shrew peering down from a second floor window, her arms folded across her chest. She is laughing at his sight.

Benton removes the bottle from his lips, screws the top back on, and puts it onto the passenger seat. He wants nothing more than to rage back into the condo and choke the life out of the bitch. He rubs his tender balls instead, "Fucking bitch. It's a good thing you injured the boys, otherwise I'd be ramming into you right now."

Abigail has a good laugh for herself, then gets down to business. She goes to her desk, pulls a wooden block from her desk drawer, and reads the name on the back, "Malcolm Price. **You** are the first order of business. I am going to find your secrets, Mr. Price, then I'm going to use them to destroy you."

Mother

Bertha King Price sits on the front stoop of her row house at 11-B Cross Street, Lewisburg, enjoying the last few minutes of fresh air before night sends her behind locked doors. Set upon her lap is that day's edition of *Liberty Rings*. She hasn't read it yet; she'll do that when she's inside. "I hope these damned papers start telling the good about my boy. It's time they let him and that poor girl be at peace."

The mother of Malcolm Price hopes she never sees things in that paper that are better left in the past. She shakes her head because she knows it's just a matter of time before someone goes looking for answers about Malcolm's father.

Father

Curtis Robert Morgan sits on the porch of his home on Skidaway Island, Georgia, enjoying the last few minutes of fresh air before night sends him behind closed doors. Folded in his hand is that day's edition of *Liberty Rings*. He has read it, cover to cover, and will do so again when he's inside. "These damned papers are tearing that man apart. They'll never leave him or that poor girl in peace."

The father of Malcolm Price hopes he never sees things in that paper that are better left in the past. He shakes his head because he knows it's just a matter of time before someone goes looking for answers about Malcolm's father.

Georgia Historical Society (GHS)
1981

Bertha King Price was standing amongst the most important collection of historical documents in all of Georgia. This was the third 'alone visit' she'd made to the Georgia Historical Society, and she was beginning to feel as though she belonged in the hallowed halls.

The first time Bertha stepped foot in GHS was when she was on a high school field trip, attending the Society's *Georgia History Festivals*. She was plumb excited about the day and listened intently to her teacher, "The mission of the Festival is to introduce visitors to the rich history of one of the first 13 colonies of the United States. Hopefully, the *Festival* will inspire you to explore Georgia's past and help you with your term paper on our great State."

The *Festival's* mission was a success—for Bertha King Price, that is. Over the past year she had explored Georgia's past at the Society's Research Center and at its Educational Center, whenever she could. That day in 1981, she was held captive by artifacts that told the story of her home state: documents, manuscripts, photographs, maps and newspapers—they filled every inch of the building—and Bertha's curiosity, until…

"Nothing in this great place documents life at Sackville. Guess Georgia's slums ain't worth commemorating," she chuckled to herself.

"What's so funny?" a voice came from behind Bertha. She turned a bit too quickly; thankful for the hands of a handsome young man who halted her fall.

"I wasn't doing anything wrong," Bertha stammered. "I was just thinking, is all."

"This is a good place for thinking. Right now, I'm thinking I'd like to know your name," he smiled warmly.

"Bertha King Price, and who might you be?" She smiled warmly.

"I am Curtis Robert Morgan. It's a pleasure to meet you Miss Price," the young man bent at the waist in formal introduction. "You know, Miss Price, I was a tour guide in these halls when I was in high school. If you would oblige me, I would appreciate the opportunity to step back into that role."

"Very well, Mr. Morgan."

He looked in several directions, "Is your interest in the people, places, or things of the great State of Georgia?"

"People."

"There are countless from which to choose, perhaps Abraham Baldwin, who served the State of Georgia as a U.S. senator and was a signatory of the Constitution of the United States; or maybe Flannery O'Connor, a Savannah-born author who lived a short time, but left a lasting literary legacy." Curtis dipped low and whispered, "I'm no fan of her short story, *A Good Man is Hard to Find*," he shook his head, "but her other works are quite good," he paused for another look around, "or perhaps Jackie Robinson is of your fancy."

Bertha stopped and asked, "The baseball player?"

"Yes, Miss Price, Mr. Robinson hails from Georgia's Wiregrass country, and was not only a brilliant athlete, but he also holds claim as an important figure in the Civil Rights Movement."

For the next two hours Bertha King Price was given a personal tour of the Society. During that time she wondered often about the fine young man keeping her company. When her wondering became too much, she stopped and faced her tour guide, "One of the people I'm interested in learning about is you, Mr. Curtis Morgan."

The young man laughed, more loudly than he should have in such a reverent place, "Well, I just so happen to be an authority on that subject." He took hold of her elbow and ushered her to a carved stone bench and waited for her to sit before joining her. "I'm a recent graduate of Yale Law School, and am back in my home state preparing for the Bar exam—a beast of a thing I should note. I hope to find employment with the District Attorney's Office and enter politics when the time is right."

Bertha King Price thought Curtis Robert Morgan was as fine looking a young man as she had ever seen. He stood tall, at least 6'2", and held a somewhat lanky form. His face was white boy handsome with angular features, a broad forehead, wide cheekbones, and a strong jaw. His hair favored the color of corn, his eyes the color of caramel candy, and his lips—Bertha should stop thinking about his lips.

At the end of Bertha's tour, Curtis pointed to a plaque, "*Non Sibi, Sed Aliis* – not for self, but for others. Those words were used by Georgia's founding trustees and adopted by the Georgia Historical Society. They are the words I'm going to use as the foundation of my campaign for President of the United States."

Bertha smiled wide, "I'll be sure to offer my vote to you, Mr. Curtis Morgan." She began toward the door and stopped when he asked if she'd like to have a bite to eat. She looked at her dress— her best dress—though terribly threadbare. She shook her head *no*.

"If it would make you more comfortable eating in, we could go to my place; it's not far from here," he said kindly.

Bertha knew she shouldn't go. She went.

The young white man, and the very young black girl, walked in silence to his tiny apartment just off the Historic District. Curtis appreciated that the silence between them wasn't one of awkwardness, but rather the byproduct of Bertha's amazement of what surrounded her.

Curtis liked Bertha already. He liked her curiosity and her quest for knowledge. He mostly liked her looks. Bertha King Price was a beautiful black girl with almond colored skin, hazel eyes that favored the green tones, cropped natural hair, and cheekbones that were cut high with one push-button dimple on her left cheek. Her smile was timid, unless she was in fascination about something Curtis said or in awe of one of the books piled high in his meager living space.

The host watched from the kitchen area as Bertha finger-skimmed the books scattered haphazardly around the living room. She pointed to one, and in her best imitation of the many ladies from history she'd read about, she asked, "May I?"

He nodded, "Of course."

She picked up Walt Whitman's *Leaves of Grass* and began reading. Curtis joined her, "Are you a fan of Whitman?"

"I've never heard of him."

He tilted his head low and chuckled, "Of all the books in this room, why did you choose that one?"

"It's the only one that isn't a textbook, or a history book, or a book about legal doings. It's different, so it must be something you like to read, not something you have to read."

Curtis chuckled again, "You are very astute, Miss Price. That is my favorite book." He pointed to the couch and put their plates of tuna sandwiches and chips onto the coffee table set before it.

"It's poetry," she said.

"A collection of poetry. Whitman is referred to as the father of free verse. *Leaves of Grass* is his most controversial collection. When it was first published it was considered obscene for its overt sexuality. Perhaps you are a bit young to read it," he smiled that warm smile of his.

"I'm seventeen, well almost," she pushed back.

"Oh, well then, a woman of your advanced years is allowed to partake," he laughed. He gestured to their lunch, "Please, eat."

Bertha picked up a half sandwich, but before biting it she asked, "Why did you bring me here?"

Curtis lifted his half sandwich, "For lunch, of course." He paused, then continued, "And I hope this will be the place where we fall in love."

Bertha and Curtis became friends months before they became lovers. Nearly every Saturday, the girl from the blighted neighborhood of Sackville made her way to a tiny apartment in the Historic District of Savannah. For the first several months she read books from his personal library, he studied for the Bar exam, and over lunch she pressed him to share things he'd learned in school and travel. On the eve of her seventeenth birthday she took his hand, "Will you teach me about sex?"

"Am I your first?"

She dropped her head as though ashamed. He lifted it and ran his thumb along her cheek, "I'll be gentle."

Curtis undressed Bertha and carried her to his bed. He undressed himself, added a layer of protection, and joined his girl. Curtis was a very good teacher, and Bertha was a very good student.

One Saturday Curtis met Bertha at the door of their little love nest, "Come on, we're going places." He handed her a yellow disposable camera, "Take lots of pictures, there's a surprise waiting at the apartment when we return." That day they visited the Savannah History Museum that is housed in an old Georgia Railway passenger shed, then headed to Battlefield Memorial Park that commemorates the second bloodiest battle of the Revolutionary War, and finished the day at the Owens-Thomas House slave quarters. When they returned from their 'going places', Curtis handed his girl a photo album, "You take the pictures, I'll develop them, and together we can put them into the album the next time you visit." Then he handed her a small leatherbound calendar. "It's so you can record our life together," he said with a warm smile.

Bertha was overcome with emotion. "I am most definitely falling in love with you in this little place, Curtis Morgan."

One of Bertha's favorite days of 'going places' was the late morning trip they took to Bonaventure Cemetery located on the Wilmington River, east of Savannah. The lovers picnicked quietly beneath Spanish moss-covered ancient oak trees, each lost in thought. Bertha spent many minutes taking pictures of the 'Bird Girl' statue, while Curtis spent many minutes taking in the image of his girl. Before leaving the historic cemetery, they took a leisurely stroll and talked about a life together.

Their 'going places' were interrupted the following Saturday at Forsyth Park, near its iconic fountain, when a group of news reporters and photographers recognized Mr. Curtis Robert Morgan, son of Senator Robert Mayfield Morgan, and swarmed him.

Bertha stepped back from the commotion, unsure of the events that were unfolding. She had no idea *her* Curtis was the son of the sitting senior senator of Georgia. The shock was evident on her face in the photos that appeared in the newspapers over the following days. No one suspected the black girl in the background of the picture was acquainted with the young Mr. Curtis Robert Morgan, let alone what she had come to mean to him. Suddenly, thoughts of a future together seemed fanciful to the girl from Sackville Slums, though Curtis was still a true believer in their having one.

The Saturday after the New Year was the last day they spent together. Bertha thought about not going into Savannah, and while she was with him, she was distant and emotional. He was confused and worried.

"Bertha, talk to me," he encouraged on more than one occasion.

She tried once, only to find her words washed away by tears.

Curtis took hold of her worrying hands, "How can I help?"

"I need a few minutes to think. Alone."

Fighting his every need to stay with her, Curtis gave her time. Alone. When he returned, Bertha was gone. She'd left no note saying where she'd gone or when she'd be back. She never came back.

The abandoned man hired a private investigator the very next day, "Dolan, I need you to find someone."

"Who?"

He trusted Dolan with his truth. "Bertha King Price, she's a young—a too young girl."

Days—agonizing days—passed before Curtis heard back from the PI. "I tracked your girl to Sackville. I heard from a number of people that she up and left the slums with no explanation to anyone."

By the end of that year, Curtis had moved on from Bertha. He was an ADA with the Chatham County District Attorney's office, involved with Madison Carlisle, and moving out of his tiny apartment. On his final sweep of the love nest he'd shared with Bertha King Price, he found her small leatherbound calendar and learned the reason why she left him.

She had missed her period.

The Bus Company

Gretchen Mitchell breezes into the executive suite of her father's law firm, Mitchell and Morgan, having spent the last two hours at her favorite hair salon in downtown Philadelphia.

Her new stepmother, Faye, shoots up from behind her desk and squeals, "I love your hair. The cut and color are so daring, what made you change it up?"

Gretchen pats her baby bump, "I can't bleach it anymore because of 78, so I'm back to my original color. Besides, the time it takes straightening it every morning is time I'll be devoting to diapers and bottles. I figured it's the perfect time for a change." She runs her fingers through what's left of her hair, "Is it too short, too edgy?"

"Absolutely not!" Faye did a really good once over, "You know, Gretchen, I never realized how much you resemble Charlize Theron, especially so now with that short-do," Faye amazes, then stops when the door to Granger Mitchell's inner sanctum opens behind her.

"What's all the racket?" the lawyer asks with a wide grin. He opens his arms a mere second before his daughter lands within. "Miss Gretchen, what have you done to your hair?"

"I cut it," she says as she touches it again.

"Yes. I can see that." He pauses. The confused man looks back and forth between the women, "Are you unhappy with it?"

She smiles. "No. No. I suppose I'm having a bit of anxiety about Malcolm's impending reaction."

"Did you tell him you were going to cut it?" Faye asks.

Gretchen shakes her head, "I thought I'd surprise him."

"I suspect surprise will be his response," Granger chuckles. "Come in, Gretchen."

She addresses Faye, "Will you come with? I think I'm in need of advice."

When all are settled, Gretchen jumps into the deep end of the conversation, "Abigail Forrester is searching for ammunition to use against Malcolm. I think she is gunning for Bertha, and I think she will find some things that will hurt Malcolm very deeply."

Granger nods, "I believe your instincts are correct, Gretchen."

"You know what I'm referring to?"

"I believe I know things," he answers without really answering.

"Your father had Malcolm investigated when you started seeing him," Faye answers for her husband.

Gretchen raises an eyebrow at Faye, then turns accusatory eyes to her father. "So, that evening at the Cottage, when you said you knew all about Malcolm Price in that haughty tone of yours, you really didn't *know* all about him," she quips.

"At the time, I knew what everyone else knew, that he was arguably the best point guard to ever play basketball." He shakes his head, "Well everyone knew all of that except you, of course."

"Yes. Yes. I didn't know that my man was big shit, once upon a time."

"Biggest," Faye corrects.

Granger stops the bantering and gets down to the business at hand, "Like I was saying, I knew about 77, but like everyone else I don't know who his father is—I doubt Malcolm even knows. In the process of looking at Malcolm, I learned a few things about Bertha."

"Was she a prostitute, Daddy?"

"A call girl. Bertha and Etta Jones, the woman who lived across from her in the projects, worked for The Bus Company a sex-for-hire organization that sent girls out on calls. They gave the girls an address and a bus ticket; it was the 1980s-equivalent to today's escort service."

Gretchen pulls a deep breath. "Bertha told me once that she and Sage Finley had things in common. I thought she might be referring to this, but I didn't want to press and she chose not to elaborate." Gretchen lets her wheels spin for a few minutes, "Daddy, the information you found, was it difficult to uncover, or is it going to be easy for Abigail to find?"

"With a fair amount of digging, she will find it, Gretchen. Does Malcolm have any idea about Bertha's past, or about your snooping, or more accurately, Researcher Randy's snooping?"

"Malcolm knows nothing," Gretchen admits.

Granger walks to his daughter, takes her hands into his and pulls her to her feet, "Gretchen, it's one thing not to tell Malcolm about a new hair style, it is a completely different thing to keep secrets from him, and to dig into his personal affairs without his knowing. You need to go to him as soon as you get back and tell him what you know. Let him learn these things from someone who loves him. Otherwise, he will learn them from someone who wants to destroy him."

275

Malcolm is pulling his Land Rover into the parking garage when he sees Gretchen walking to the privacy elevator. He pulls next to her and lowers the window, "Hey sweet thing, my wife's out of town. You feel like doing me?" he smiles wide and winks.

Gretchen sashays to the car and begins to flirt, thinks better of it under the circumstances and says, "I have all the man I can handle, thanks anyway."

Malcolm rolls forward, "Don't move. I want you in that elevator."

Gretchen giggles, "Come get me, big boy." She is standing inside the polished brass box holding her thong by one finger when he races in.

He slams his gigantic hand against the close-door-button and moves her against the wall. He runs his fingers through her short, slicked back hair and presses his arousal against her. "You are stunning. I had no idea," he growls. "I'm not waiting, Charlize. I want in."

She laughs at the name.

Malcolm's words release enough excitement to let him slide right in. They've found that the beginning of her second trimester has unleashed an abundance of happy horny hormones, and she easily takes all of him. He takes her hard and fast, finishing her before the elevator doors open at the penthouse floor. "Woman, be ready later for a little gentling."

She smiles even though she knows it will be much, much later before her man gentles her again. She follows Malcolm through the penthouse; he heads to his home office, she heads to the campaign office where she finds Researcher Randy sitting on the corner of a desk, at which a young woman is doing campaign mailings.

Gretchen quickly eyes the object of Randy's attention and silently decides, *she's the millennial version of Betty Boop.* The adorable hipster chick has a softly squared face; expressively round, lushly lashed, light blue eyes;

and Cupid-bow lips. Gretchen knows the girl's first name is Peyton, that she studies at UPenn, and that she comes in on Mondays—and now she knows that Peyton has caught the eye of The Kid.

Randy hops from the desk when he sees Gretchen walk in. "Hey, Mrs. Adjacent, your 'do' is smokin.'" He turns his attention back to the girl, "This is Peyton Wells; she's UPenn like you."

Gretchen grins, "I'm aware." She smiles wide, "What's your major, Peyton?"

"I'm at Penn Law now. I graduated UPenn in May with a major/minor in political-science and history, with a focus on pre-law. I basically studied anything that will help get me to where I want to go," the girl with the bow lips tries a wide smile.

"And where do you want to go?" the very intrigued woman asks.

"The Supreme Court."

"Well, imagine that. One day I'll be able to say that Supreme Court Justice Peyton Wells helped elect my husband Mayor of Lewisburg," she says with a bright smile. "We appreciate your efforts Madam Justice." Gretchen turns to Randy, "When you have a minute."

Two minutes later Randy slides to a stop in front of Gretchen's office door, "I have that minute you wanted."

"Shut the campaign office down and don't come back until after midnight. Malcolm and I are going to be in conversation, then he's going to be unsettled."

"After midnight, Mrs. Adjacent." He steps outside her office and calls out to Peyton, "Ms. Wells, I'm heading to Si, Pizza at Merchants Square. Care to join?"

"Si, Pizza."

"Are you repeating, or accepting, Miss Wells?"

"Both."

Researcher Randy leans back in to Gretchen's office, "This girl..." he says with a smile.

Who is my father?

Gretchen has been standing outside Malcolm's office with her back pressed against a wall for many minutes. When she no longer hears him talking on the phone, she knocks.

The man behind closed doors knows the campaign office is closed—he saw Randy and the new girl leave—so he knows it's Gretchen knocking, "Woman, are we trying something new?"

Gretchen opens the door, "We need to talk," she turns and leaves. He follows, catching up to her in two gigantic steps. She takes hold of his hand and leads him to their conversation couch. "Sit." He does. She straddles his lap, takes his hand, and places it onto their baby bump. "I'm going to tell you things that are going to make you very angry. Please remember I am pregnant."

Malcolm's eyes hood. He nods.

Gretchen draws a deep breath holds it for a second, then lets it go. "When you and I had words over Sage, a while back, and I took off my engagement ring, Mama Girl came to talk to me. During that conversation things were said." She pulls a shaky breath, lets it out slowly, "Mama Girl had just lectured you about truth-telling, and she knew I had questions about Sage. So she told me to ask the burning questions—then she set me straight that she would tell the full truth, so to only ask what I could handle."

Gretchen pauses.

"Woman, talk to me."

"The first question I asked was what Sage was like. Mama Girl said she never met the girl, but she knew her deep. She said Sage was like Mama Girl was at a similar age, pregnant, alone, and doing what she needed to do to survive." Gretchen takes a breath in. Gretchen lets a breath out. "Then Mama Girl said that women do what needs to be done using what they have. She gave me a look that has stuck with me."

Malcolm shifts a bit. Gretchen stays firm on his lap.

"Since your WNEP interview, I have had the feeling that Abigail Forrester is going to go after Mama Girl in order to try to find out who your father is. The paternity issue may be problematic; we won't know if that is the case until we know who your father is. I fear the more immediate problem is Mama Girl. I asked Randy to start digging into your parents, then I had better thoughts on the subject."

Malcolm shifts a lot. Gretchen presses firmly on his lap.

"When I was in Philly today, I stopped in to see Daddy. I told him Abigail Forrester is searching for ammunition to use against you and that I think she is gunning for Bertha. I also told him Abigail may find some things that will hurt you very deeply."

Malcolm stops moving and stares nearly through her.

Gretchen picks up the pace, "Daddy nodded and said my instincts are correct. Apparently, when you and I began our relationship, Granger Mitchell had you looked into, and he learned things about your mother."

Malcolm gently, but with purpose, lifts Gretchen off his lap and puts her onto the couch. He makes his way to a wall across the room. He leans back. He says nothing for several minutes, "Are you finished, Gretchen?"

She shakes her head, "I asked Daddy if Mama Girl was a prostitute. He said she was a call girl. He said Mama Girl and a woman named Etta Jones, worked for The Bus Company, a sex-for-hire organization that sent girls out on calls. They were given an address and a bus ticket. Daddy said it was the 1980s version of an escort service." A breath in. A breath out. "I didn't want to tell you, Malcolm. I'm sorry I had to."

"Wasn't your story to tell, and you're not the one who should be sorry. I'll be back."

11-B Cross Street
Bertha King Price hears Malcolm's Land Rover screech to the curb in front of her little row house. She knows why he's come. She meets

him at the door, "Come on in boy, there's some talkin' ahead of us." When he walks past her, Bertha feels a boiling fury in her son—it is something she's never sensed before. "Sit down boy, and you hold your anger and your judgments to yourself. I did what I did and what little I owe for my choices, I'll rightly pay."

Malcolm moves across the room from his Mama Girl and presses his back tight against the wall. He could say any measure of things—could ask any number of things—none that really matter much. To Malcolm there is only one question of any consequence, "Who is my father?"

"Can't say, Malcolm."

"Can't say because you don't know?"

"I know who your father is. There was deep love between us when we made you. That's all I can say. You should take that and let it ease your mind."

Malcolm scoffs. "If there was love between the two of you, why did you leave him? You need to tell me. People are digging, and they are going to find out about…you," he intentionally inflicts some pain with his words. The hurting man quiets himself some, then asks his mother the burning question. "Why did you leave my father?"

"To protect him," she tears.

"From?"

"Himself. The man loved me to distraction. He shouldn't have. He was twenty-eight and I was seventeen. My pregnancy would have put him in jail. Certainly, would have caused him and his family scandal. I loved him enough to leave."

Malcolm lowers his voice and tone. "He never helped you?" The son loses a bit of his anger, replaces it with pity for his mother.

"He never knew."

"He must know now, I'm goddamn famous and you by extension," the rage is back. "Mama Girl, I'm gonna ask again and understand this, I will find out who he is. I'd like you to respect me like I'm respecting you right now." Malcolm let his words find his Mama Girl's core. "Who. Is. My. Father?"

Mama Girl tears at the thought of speaking the man's name after all these years. She begins shaking and gently rocks herself to and fro. Malcolm goes to her and kneels at her feet. He takes her hands in his, "Mama Girl, please."

When Bertha King Price is ready, she puts her hands on her boy's face, musters up the courage and proudly says, "Your father is Senator Curtis Robert Morgan of the great State of Georgia."

Malcolm hangs his head low. In the silent moments that follow, he places the image of Senator Morgan into the fatherly void he's carried within him. The long held boyish desire for a father is harshly pushed aside by the ramifications of this news, "When this secret is revealed, two political careers may be over," he says as he pushes up and walks away from his Mama Girl.

When he gets to the Land Rover, he realizes that he didn't hug his mother goodbye. He has always hugged his Mama Girl goodbye.

The son heads back to his mother's house and into her waiting arms.

Devastated and disgusted daughters.

Penny Meehan is a woman who takes care of herself. Orphaned at the age of six, she's had many years of experience in that department...

Young Penny eased onto the last step of the school bus. She took hold of the handrail and leaned forward, peering out past the two people standing just outside, waiting for her. When her feet sort of slid off the final step onto the ground, Mrs. Dombrowski took hold of her hand to help right her.

"Where's Mommy?" the little girl whimpered, already knowing, certainly sensing that something was wrong—terribly wrong. The Dombrowski's had never given any indication that they knew Penny existed, and now they were here, meeting her school bus. "Where's Daddy?" the little girl began to cry.

"You need to come with us, Penny."

The little girl looked back at the bus driver who offered a small smile then pulled the big handle that closed the bus door.

Penny had always been told by her parents to be seen and not heard. She followed their directive when they were alive—and even more so when the Dombrowski's became her guardians, but when she turned eighteen and moved out of the gated community that held the secrets to what happened to her parents, Penny became very vocal about her plans…

"I don't know what happened to my mother and father, but I promise you both I will find out." Those were the last words Penny Meehan spoke to Mr. and Mrs. Dombrowski.

The vow she made that day is why she went into journalism. It is why she no longer follows her mother's directive to be seen and not heard. It is also why the woman makes an impression when she enters a room. If she isn't calling attention by something she's saying, then her body does the talking for her. Penny Meehan is 5'8" tall, has ramrod straight posture and a frame of all lean muscle. She wears her black hair shorn very short, and her dark brown almond-shaped eyes crinkle along the edges whenever she smiles. The thing is, Penny doesn't smile all that much, so those smile crinkles are unlikely to turn into wrinkles anytime soon.

The impatient reporter is sitting in her 3'x5' cubicle, waiting for her newsroom colleagues to leave. Her fingers tap anxiously along the desktop, and one of her legs shakes out nervous energy, "Gooooo home," she encourages the day shifters on a whisper. "I need to put some time into researching Bertha King Price. Come on. Go home." Penny needs the prying eyes of people who are paid to have prying eyes to leave. Night shifters are due in at any minute, but Penny knows they consider her nothing more than a blight on their profession; she's certainly not someone they should be monitoring. After all, what scoop could a former trash reporter get? "Let's see how they feel about me when I break the story of the year—maybe the decade," she gloats.

The increasingly anxious snoop keeps an eye on her boss, careful not to rouse his suspicion. "Don't need to involve you in my little research project Mr. Geist. I've already suffered through one of your ass-reamings over the Sage Finley debacle—no desire to repeat that experience, sir." At the umpteenth whoosh of air, signaling the close of the newsroom door, the woman takes a peek around the corner of her office space. She. Is. Alone. She plops back onto her chair, swivels to her computer, and keys Bertha King Price into a search engine. "The only information I have about you Bertha, is that you're from Savannah and you were born in 1965. It's not much to go on, but I have a nose for smut and my nose is twitching—big time."

Philly
Abigail Forrester is in her home office playing with her blocks. It's her favorite place to be—her favorite thing to do. She takes the Malcolm Price block out of the desk drawer and passes it from

hand to hand while she plots and plans. She places it on top of her Tower of Power, "Well, **that** was unsatisfying." She pulls a long breath, "This Price-imposed detour is fucking with my head." She moves to her window and peers out for many minutes until she settles on a thought, "I need a little inspiration." She heads to a filing cabinet across the room, opens a drawer, pulls a file, marches back to her desk, and begins reading the capstone report she did during her senior year at Blakesville College…

People of Pennsylvania:
There's More to Life Than Coal!
By: Abigail Forrester
A Fricken Coal Miner's Daughter

For centuries, a big swath of northeast Pennsylvania, located in the central Ridge-and-Valley parts of the Appalachian Mountains, has been known as Coal Country. The people who live in the anthracite rich communities of Lackawanna, Luzerne, Columbia, Carbon, Schuykill, and Northumberland counties hold fast to their mining way of life. Generations of coal miners and their families have lived and died for coal.

For personal reasons—some might say, for pathological reasons—Abigail Forrester is hell bent on ripping coal from the blackened hands of Pennsylvania miners. She isn't one of "those" people who objects to mining because of the negative effects on the land, water, and air.

Abigail couldn't give a lick about any of those trivial things. She wants to decimate the coal industry because she fucking hates coal—and everyone—and everything—associated with it.

Growing up in Scranton, Abigail heard endless stories about the look, weight, and grade of anthracite coal. By the time she was five, she would be put on display to recite coal names at family gatherings...

"Abigail, it's coal time," her mother would say.

Abigail, the delightfully dutiful daughter, would stand front and center and perform her recitation, "Black coal, hard coal, and stone coal is from the United States. Dark coal, coffee coal, and blind coal is from Scotland. Crow coal, craw coal, and black diamond coal is from Ireland..."

The little girl from Scranton heard, ad nauseam, how her hometown is what it is because of coal, how it became incorporated because of its mining and railroads, how Theodore Roosevelt, himself, settled the 1902 anthracite coalminer strike, and how Scranton became known as the capital of the anthracite coal industry. Yet, in all the droning on about coal, Abigail never once heard about the problems associated with coal mining. She learned about those while researching for her college term paper...

...Sub-surface mining weakened Scranton neighborhoods, causing the collapse of land beneath them; it created ghost towns, like in Centralia, where an underground fire has been burning in the mines since 1962. Mining resulted in thousands of accidents, and countless deaths from the disease known as black lung.

A reenergized Abigail walks the report back to the filing cabinet reminding herself along the way, "The most important thing I learned about coal is that I fucking hate it. Once I get Topher Griffin seated as the next Governor of the Commonwealth of Pennsylvania, he and I will replace coal mining with natural gas fracking. He'll fatten his coffers with tens of millions, and I will run the state any damn way I see fit. All I need to do is get Malcolm Price out of the way."

God dammit, all!

Gretchen wakes to an empty bed and immediately goes in search of her man—it is an abbreviated search. She finds Malcolm sitting on the conversation couch staring off into space. She stands at the doorway unsure what to do— he clears things up for her, "Not now, Gretchen."

The worried wife is at the bank of windows overlooking Hufnagle when her unsettled husband heads toward her. He has an overnight bag slung over his shoulder, "I'll be back in a couple days." He cups his hand at the back of her head and pulls her for a kiss, "You and I are good, Woman. Don't worry." He wipes a lone tear that slides down her cheek, "I'll be back. Take care of 78. I love you."

Malcolm sets his GPS to take him where he needs to go, then lets his mind take him wherever it damn well pleases...

"Before you sign that national letter of intent to play, you need to unburden me some."

Malcolm knew what was wearing on his Mama Girl, "I **want** to study history and play ball at Bucknell."

"You could go anywhere, son."

"I'll go anywhere when I turn pro. Truth, Mama Girl, leaving you would burden me some."

~

The recent college graduate sat on the front stoop of his Mama Girl's row house at 11-B Cross Street in Lewisburg, Pennsylvania. From the front room of the house, the steady drone of talking heads was annoying the young man deep to his bones, but he listened. After all, one of those two sports announcers would eventually call his name and that of the team he'd be playing for.

"Sit tight players. This is gonna be a l.o.n.g. night."

"Right you are, Don. The 2003 NBA draft roster might just have the most talented pool in draft history. We already know that the first selection this evening will go to Cleveland. Chairman Gordon Gund announced in May that the Cavs will pick LeBron James, so there'll be no surprise there. The second and third selections will go to the Detroit Pistons and the Denver Nuggets, and there's lots of speculation about who they will pull, then..."

"...then it will get really interesting, and I suspect frustrating for the players. And these PLAYERS—any one of them could have been the first round pick: Marquette's Dwayne Wade, and Georgia Tech's Chris Bosh, and Georgetown's Michael

Sweetney, and Bucknell's Malcolm Price, and Xavier's David West, and ..."

Malcolm tossed the rock he'd been flipping from hand to hand, watched it skip across the street and drop through a sewer grate. He got up from the stoop, climbed four concrete stairs, and pressed his back tight against the wall by the screen door. With each player's name called, his head hung a little lower and his hands clenched a little tighter.

"And the number ten slot goes to..."
"And the number twenty slot goes to..."
"And it looks like Malcolm Price is headed to..."

~

Gretchen moved from her end of the couch and nestled between Malcolm's outstretched legs, leaned back against him and wrapped his arms around, "It's your turn. Tell me about your family."

"It's just me and my mother, Bertha King Price of Savannah, Georgia. Our mothers hail from the same state. Different circumstances, though. Mama Girl, I call her that because she is my mama, but she had me when she was still a girl of seventeen."

Gretchen smiled, "Well isn't that just wonderful!"

He smiled and continued, "I don't know who my father is, but I know he is Caucasian, is considerably older than Bertha, and from a 'different station in life' than Mama Girl. She left Georgia without telling her family about me, and I'm not sure if she told the man who impregnated her. Whatever her reasoning, Bertha Price put her belongings into a brown paper bag and boarded a bus to the home of the Liberty Bell. Problem was, she couldn't remember where the Bell was located, so she ended up in Lewisburg. I'm sure that part of Mama Girl's story is fiction. My mother is a learner of history, so I suspect there is another reason why she ended up in Lewisburg. Mama Girl and I lived for many years in a fifth-floor walk-up in the projects. We had no family to help us out, so Mama Girl created a family for us. Miss Etta Jones, a single mother of three lived across the hall from us. She and Mama Girl traded off on childcare so they could earn a paycheck. Mama Girl watched me and Etta's kids during the day and then worked as a secretary at the bus company at night while I stayed at Etta's place. A bonus for Mama Girl was that her boss gave her free bus passes that she and Etta used to get back and forth to work and she and I would use to get to Sunday morning services. By the time I began high school, Mama Girl had enough money to buy a tiny row house. It's in the roughest section of The Burg, but it's her home. I don't like her living there, but as she reminds me, it's none of my never mind."

"The Bus Company." He gives his head a good shaking before repeating the words and adding a few, "The Bus Company. Secrets sure have their way of comin' round."

Savannah, Georgia
Malcolm calls Hannah Leavy, a cyber specialist at Rocco Fiancetti Incorporated, for an assist. "I need the private phone number for Senator Curtis Robert Morgan."

"On it Malcolm," Leavy says without questioning why he needs it.

Within minutes, a son calls a father for the first time, "This is Malcolm Price. Is this a good time, Senator? I'm in Savannah." The senator gives Malcolm the address of his home on Skidaway Island.

The senator is pacing along the shore of Moon River when he hears a car pull up. He walks a cobbled path toward the man he recognizes as 77 and extends his hand, "The minute you announced your candidacy, I knew this meeting was forthcoming."

Malcolm nods.

"Come on, let's get to it," the senator says in words that could have come from Mama Girl's mouth.

Malcolm waits until they are behind closed doors of the senator's home office, "The timing of this meeting is unfortunate, but time is of the essence, so I'd appreciate your answering the questions I have, and I'll be on my way."

The senator nods.

"When did you first learn that you are my father?"

"In 2003, when you turned pro. I read an article on you and it mentioned Bertha's name."

"Did my mother tell you about the pregnancy?"

The man pulls a deep breath and releases it slowly. "Sadly, no. On our last day together, Bertha was troubled by something. She asked for some time alone, and like a damned fool, I gave it to her. When I returned to our place, she was gone. I hired a private investigator who tracked her to the Sackville projects. People who knew her said she was long gone. A year after she left me, I was moving out of the apartment where she and I spent our time. I found a calendar she used to document our lives together—apparently, she documented her menstrual cycle in that calendar, too. That's the day I found out about the missed period. Instead of telling me about the pregnancy, she ran."

"And in 2003, when I went pro, did you think about contacting us?"

The man nods, then shakes his head. "At that time, I was Congressman out of the 1st District of Georgia with my sights set on becoming senator. I had my private investigator take a look into your lives. Dolan learned some things about your mother..." the senator stops and looks at Malcolm, unsure if he should continue.

"Senator, I know of those things. Speak freely."

"I'm not shielding you from those things, Malcolm. I'm shielding myself from thinking about all of the things Bertha did to support you and to protect me."

Malcolm wades into the unsettled waters, "What did my mother protect you from?"

"Myself. I would have given everything I had, or ever would have, for Bertha."

Malcolm scoffs, "She said those exact words about you."

"Because they are true. Your mother left me that day because had our illicit affair become known, it would have cost me everything, perhaps even my freedom. Instead of letting me suffer the consequences of my actions, she left me with everything and took nothing in return." The senator stares at his Moon River, "I was allowed to have all of this because your mother loved me."

Malcolm allows the man his quiet moments of reflection and takes a few for himself. He walks the room, surveying pieces of a personal and professional history all richly framed and proudly displayed: educational degrees, congressional and senatorial headshots, newspaper articles of note, and family photographs. The man with no paternal history leans in and studies a picture of Senator Curtis Robert Morgan standing with his father, Senator Robert Mayfield Morgan. Malcolm recognizes the smile on the men's faces as his own. *My blood*, he silently reflects and accepts. He strolls back toward the fine reproduction of the writing desk used by President George Washington upon which sits two things: a bumper sticker that reads, **Curtis Morgan for President – 2020** and a copy of *Liberty Rings*.

"Senator, what about your plans? Will you still run for President?"

The senator shakes his head, "Not likely." He ignores that bitter pill, concentrating instead on the issues at hand, "Take a seat Malcolm and ask your questions."

"Senator, you said you knew this talk was forthcoming."

"Politics is an awful business, Malcolm, a blood sport, really. You have had a taste of what's in store with the whole Sage Finley matter, but do not delude yourself into thinking the worst is behind you. Every stone you have set as your foundation, every wall you have built for your protection, will be pulled up and toppled over by those in search of a mistake in judgment, or tawdry tidbit, or moral misstep you've made along the way. You have answered the noble call of public service. In doing so you have offered yourself up to scrutiny.

Unfortunately, the forces who want to dirty you up won't stop with you; they will focus on the people you love. They are going to set their sights on Bertha, the single mother who raised a son on the poverty-ridden streets of Lewisburg. They will keep after her until they find out why the two of you were on your own. What they will really be after is finding out who your father is. That missing piece mattered some when you were playing ball, but it is all that matters now that you're running for office. When the hounds learn that the sitting senior senator of Georgia is your father, they are going to come gunning for me. God knows I've given them enough ammunition. I slept with an underage black girl. It won't matter how deeply I loved her; that revelation alone will end my political aspirations. More importantly, the fallout from that scandal will affect the only two women I have ever loved. Bertha will be raked over the coals and vilified by people who want me to become President. They will see her as the reason I am not. My wife, Madison, who knows nothing of you and Bertha, will be forced to deal with my private failings in a very public way. Madison and I never had children, a wound that runs deep in her. Now, she will learn that I fathered a child with another woman. The life Madison and I have built and the dreams of my becoming President will be gone." He swivels his chair toward Moon River and finishes, "Worst of all, I won't be able to protect any of us from the vitriolic attacks that will come," the senator ends, defeat heavy in his words.

"Senator, let me repeat what I said when I first arrived, time is of the essence. There is someone gunning for information to use against me and when she learns you are my father, she will make it her life's mission to destroy us, both."

"Her name?"

"Abigail Forrester."

Senator Curtis Robert Morgan shoots from his chair and slams his hands onto his desk, "God dammit all!"

It must be genetic.

The senator takes another trip to the windows and silently watches a fading sun cast its final bit of light on the river he loves. He takes his fill, then returns to the problem at hand. "Abigail Forrester is a calculating, manipulative, albeit brilliant woman, who has eaten her fair share of weak men and who is readying herself to spit them back out." He returns to his desk, "Pardon my bluntness, but if Abigail is gunning for you, you'd better expect a bullet to your ass. She comes loaded for bear and never misses her mark."

"Care to elaborate?"

"I first met Abigail Forrester in the late 1990s when she was interning in the office of Congressman Turner Rodgers out of the former 17th District of Pennsylvania. The damned fool thought his dalliance with the intern was all fun and games until Abigail got the goods on him. I don't know what she found, but I know it was big enough for him to put her through Georgetown University. Abigail Forrester will have a party for herself when she learns I can't run on the Democratic ticket because of this scandal. She harbors deep resentment for me because I rebuffed her wanton attempts way-back-when. More to the point, the vengeful woman still has the blackmail weapon she used against Turner Rodgers. She's going to pull that weapon free and use it against one of the most powerful men in the world—all to advance her goals. Mark my words, Malcolm, if there is a President Rodgers sitting in the Oval Office come next November, there will be an Abigail Forrester sitting next to him."

Malcolm's head starts throbbing.

The senator continues. "When Abigail was in graduate school, she spent plenty of time digging for dirt on elected officials on the Hill. Again, I don't know what she has, but I know who hides behind closed doors when she's around. When she left DC in the early 2000s, and went out on her own, she started working **way** below her credentials and her political savvy. She spent her time in Pennsylvania counties, townships, and boroughs like Lewisburg, instead of heading to Harrisburg, your state's center of political power."

"Any idea why?"

"My guess is it has something to do with consolidations and mergers."

Malcolm's head starts pounding.

Senator Morgan stops talking at a knock upon his door, "Come in, Madison, I'd like you to meet someone," he says as he heads to greet his wife and escort her inside.

Malcolm is introduced to a beautiful biracial woman. Madison is light skinned, wears her black hair cut short and straightened, her eyes are olive green and warm, and her cheeks are cut high. Her smile is wide and full of affection.

"Madison, this is Malcolm Price. You certainly know him as 77, the best damned point guard to ever play basketball."

Madison extends her hand to Malcolm, but addresses her husband, "I know him as your son, too, Curtis."

Malcolm's head explodes.
Curtis' head explodes.
It must be genetic.

"Malcolm, it is a pleasure to meet you. I am going to make this visit short and leave you two men to the task of gathering your slack jaws together. Curtis, I'm sure you and I will be discussing this issue in full at a later time. While Malcolm is in Savannah, I expect him to dine with us and spend the night, if time allows." Madison kisses her husband's cheek and lightly touches Malcolm's arm on the way out.

Malcolm pulls his slack jaw together then quickly opens it again, "Is she for real?"

Curtis Morgan shakes his head, "I've been wondering that same thing for nearly 37 years."

Madison directs her dinner guest to a table set on a magnificent wrap-porch facing Moon River. "I have a few things of weight to get off my chest. They are directed at the both of you, so I'd like quiet until I've finished speaking." Madison waits.

The men nod their assent.

"Curtis Robert Morgan, you will run for president if that is what you are called to do. I know you two are thinking the situations at hand are politically insurmountable, but that is pure nonsense. When Curtis entered politics, Malcolm, he and I dealt with whatever issues people have with white and black relations. Granted, I am a fair-skinned black woman, which makes me a bit more palatable for some, but put my family nearby and everyone knows I am a black woman.

"As for Bertha's choices, they may cause concern for some of the older voters, but Bertha did what she needed to do for her son. And what a fine son she raised. Malcolm Price is a man who made much of himself, and who now wants to give back by serving the community in which he lives. This current scandal has nothing to do with Malcolm Price, and I predict he won't suffer political consequences for it. I expect the people who loved him as 77 aren't likely to vote against him—it would be akin to betting against the hometown boy when he played for the Spurs.

"As for the age difference between Curtis and Bertha. This is the most concerning issue. Senator Curtis Morgan will take a hit on this, but being an established, scandal-free, principled public servant, this will be nothing more than fodder for the gossip mill until something more salacious comes along. Curtis, I suggest you take full ownership of the situation, then watch the polls and see what happens. If things swing in your favor and you go toe-to-toe against Turner Rodgers in the general election, you'll have leveled the playing field, but not by much. My advice to you both is to get out ahead of this. Schedule a news conference; make the announcement yourselves. Taking the wind out of a ship's sails is the best way to keep it from crashing."

Madison leaves the porch to get dinner and drinks.

Malcolm looks at his father and asks, for the second time that day, "Is she for real?"

The evening Malcolm spends with Curtis and Madison Morgan is one of the most enjoyable he's had. Talk turns from politics—to family—to basketball—with ease.

Madison gently touches Malcolm's arm, "Curtis attended his fair share of Spurs games during your playing years." Malcolm is rewarded by a prideful look in his father's eyes. "He was at the Final Championship game in 2007, against the Cleveland Cavaliers," Madison finishes.

A memory pushes in…

The Malcolm Price was against the wall. His focus was gone, his tempo was off, his patience was thin, and his temper was shot to shit. One more penalty and he'd be tossed from the game. He sprinted to the sideline, took a seat, and worked on settling himself. Something in the stands caught his eye—*someone* in the stands caught his eye—a tall, distinguished man in jeans and a tweed sport coat was leaning against a wall, his feet crossed at the ankles, his eyes drilling 77. The man nodded. The buzzer broke Malcolm's stare and called him back to the game. His game. The one he refused to lose.

Malcolm hangs his head, "That was one of the worst games of my career. Just awful."

"You won. That's what I remember," Curtis says.

"My team won," the former b-baller reminds.

"A team is like a campaign, and a point guard is like a candidate. He or she controls the offense and sets the tempo of the ultimate game—politics. No matter how hard the people around a point guard or candidate work, everyone knows who the driving force is."

Malcolm smirks and shakes his head, "I think I've fallen into my wife's rabbit hole."

"Come again?" Curtis asks.

"Can't be explained, but when you meet Gretchen it will be understood," he says with a wide, near-painful grin.

"Malcolm, do you and Gretchen know the gender of your baby?" Madison practically purrs the question.

"No, ma'am, but I sure do hope it's a girl and that she favors my wife."

Curtis clears his throat, "Malcolm, I know Gretchen's father, Granger. He and I were classmates at Yale Law."

Madison spins out of Curtis's embrace, "Oh, my goodness, Granger Mitchell is Gretchen's father? Well, that bit of information slipped under my radar. I don't know your father-in-law, Malcolm, but I have heard his name a time or two. Oh, well, this is all so familial already. Men, get on that announcement, so we can unite our families and move them forward."

As Curtis leads his house guest upstairs, Malcolm asks a burning question, "Is Madison in politics?"

Curtis laughs, "She's my campaign manager, always has been, always will be."

Malcolm returns the laugh, "Gretchen is my campaign manager."

"Then, she will see you to victory, son."

Malcolm smiles w.i.d.e. at the reference.

Epic orgasms.

Malcolm calls Granger on the drive home from Georgia and asks that he and Faye gather the troops for a family meeting at 275, that afternoon.

Gretchen, Mama Girl, Granger, Faye and Researcher Randy are sharing a raucous laugh when the privacy elevator door opens to deliver the returning wanderer. Not one of those assembled stops their frivolity, in fact, they break into a whole new round of laughter. Malcolm steps just inside the door and counts his blessings. He drops his bag, waves to everyone and walks to his wife, "Come with me." Malcolm takes Gretchen's hand and leads her to their bedroom. "Woman, one hour with them," he tosses his head in the direction of his gathered family. "Then I'm going to gentle you all night." He kisses her on the top of her head and leaves the room.

Gretchen quickly follows, "Okay, listen up! Malcolm has something to say, then you will all say your piece—keep them abbreviated and succinct. And then you will leave. We are on the clock, so."

Malcolm interrupts his wife, "Slow your roll, Woman."

Researcher Randy gets up to leave, "I'll be in the campaign office if this family talk-train goes off the rails."

Malcolm points to a seat, "Kid, sit. You're family."

Five sets of eyes turn to Malcolm. He smiles wide. "Two nights ago, Mama Girl told me who my father is. I went to see him." Malcolm looks at his mother; she smiles and nods. Silence and stillness capture the room; the man who owns it begins again. "Granger you know my father, he was a classmate of yours at Yale Law." Malcolm leaves his words hanging and watches Granger's face for any sign of recognition. It comes.

"I'll. Be. Damned. You're Curtis Morgan's son."

Gretchen's head practically swings free from her neck as her attention leaves her father and moves toward her husband. "Senator Curtis Morgan? From the state of Georgia? Where Savannah is located? Oh. My. God." Gretchen's head swings in the other direction, "Mama Girl?"

"I'll handle this, Mama Girl," Malcolm directs. "When my mother got pregnant, Curtis Morgan was twenty-eight and she was seventeen. She knew that if the news became public, Curtis would face jail time. At the very least there would be a scandal involving the son of sitting Senator Robert Mayfield Morgan. She ran without telling my father she was pregnant."

He turns to his mother, "Curtis hired a private investigator to find you when you first left. Nearly a year later, when he was moving out of his apartment, he found your calendar and learned of the pregnancy. At that time he was working at the District Attorney's office and was involved with Madison Carlisle. He said he'd searched once for the young girl he loved, with no success, so he put his past in the past and moved on with Madison."

Mama Girl nodded, and teared.

"In 2003, when I went pro, he read an article about me and saw that Bertha King Price was my mother. He was a state Congressman by then and was looking at a run for Senate. He had the private investigator look into us and..." Malcolm pauses.

"And he learned of my past," Mama Girl finishes her son's sentence for him. "What that man must think," the anguished woman says with her head hung low.

Malcolm kneels at his mother's feet, "What he thinks is that your love for him was beyond all measure. He recognizes the sacrifice you made for him and is humbled by it. That man loved you right fine, Bertha King Price."

Malcolm touches his mother shoulder, leaves it there until her head find its way back up.

"There's much more to this story, but I need to address the important things. Senator

Curtis Morgan is contemplating a run for president. Obviously, all of this puts his political aspirations, and to a lesser extent my aspirations, in jeopardy. His wife, Madison, a perfectly wonderful woman and an inspired campaign manager, suggests the two of us hold a press conference and make our announcement. Curtis and I have agreed. They have invited us to their home this weekend to strategize. The press conference will be held Sunday. All we need to do is keep this quiet for a few days."

Within the hour of Malcolm's return home, he has his wife pressed against the shower. He runs his fingers through her cropped hair, "Woman I loved the sassy swing of your platinum hair, but this is fucking hot."

Gretchen smiles so wide her cheeks hurt.

They crawl into bed. Malcolm spends many, many minutes kissing his wife. He pulls himself from the taste that was made for him and heads to the taste he craves. He works his woman to her edge, then pulls himself up and lays next to her. "I need you on top. I want to look at you when you tighten around me. Take what you can, Woman. Don't hurt yourself."

Gretchen straddles her man and eases in the length of him. He touches her as she gently rides him. She lowers her chest to his as a powerful orgasm grips her. He holds her close as she struggles to come down—waits for her hold to loosen. Her waves of release continue in an unfamiliar way—he loses himself inside her.

Gretchen stays perfectly still on his chest.

"Talk to me, Woman."

She begins to quiver, and her breathing becomes erratic. She's almost panting as Malcolm lifts her from him and gently rolls her onto her back. She moans, but seems unconnected to the space she fills. Slowly, Gretchen comes down and around.

"Woman, what the hell?"

"Oh. My. God. That was un-fuck-ing-believable." Gretchen starts shivering and laughing.

"Woman, I don't think I've ever heard you cuss. What's going on?"

"I think I just had one of **those** pregnancy orgasms I've read about. They. Are. Intense. It has something to do with blood being in all the right places, enhanced by an extra boost of adrenaline. I don't exactly know all there is to know about them, but I know I want another one, please."

Malcolm shakes his head, "I thought I killed you, Woman."

Gretchen starts to crawl onto him, "Please kill me again," she laughs. Malcolm growls, "If it's all the same to you, I'd rather gentle you some."

Malcolm gentles his woman
to another epic pregnancy orgasm.

I know what we are having.

Gretchen calls Malcolm from her ob-gyn appointment to say she's being sent for an ultrasound. Her call goes directly to voicemail. She tries him again right before she lies back on the exam table.

"Why am I having this ultrasound?" she asks the sonographer, who answers the question without really answering the question.

"Your measurement markers are a bit off."

Measurement markers, Gretchen ponders. "Oh, the tape measured size of my baby bump?" the mom-to-be asks.

"Yes. Among other things."

"When you say the markers are a bit off, are they on the bigger or smaller side?"

"Bigger," the technician says with a reassuring smile.

Gretchen stops talking and starts looking at the monitor when she hears a rapid beating sound. She gasps when she sees 78 for the first time. Mom is transfixed by the image of her baby and momentarily forgets why she's there.

The technician manipulates the doppler, freezes the image on the computer monitor, takes a series of photos that go directly to a printer and asks, "Do you want to know the sex of your baby?"

"Yes!" Gretchen says before a second's thought.

She is dressed and staring at the very first picture of her baby when the doctor comes into the examination room.

"Okay, Ms. Mitchell, based on your physical examination and the ultrasound results your due date is in early January."

Gretchen processes that for a second, "This baby was conceived in April. Malcolm gentled me for the first time in April. This baby was meant to be," she whispers.

"Come again," the doctor encourages.

Gretchen changes course. "The baby's father is 6'5". Could that affect the size of my baby?"

"When you deliver, perhaps." The doctor pats her knee with a 'good luck with that' look on his face and leaves.

Gretchen finds Malcolm in the bedroom packing for the upcoming weekend at Senator Morgan's home. She leans against the doorjamb, "Why didn't you answer my calls, or return them?"

Malcolm pats his pockets looking for his cell, "What calls, Woman?"

"I was at the ob-gyn, and they sent me for an ultrasound."

Malcolm moves toward her, "Is everything okay?"

Gretchen turns and walks away.

He follows her to the game room where she points to their conversation couch, "Sit."

He does.

She waves the ultrasound picture back and forth in the air, "This is a picture of 78. The doctor said our baby will be here in early January."

Malcolm springs from the couch, "Woman, you had me worked a bit. Are you feeling okay? Is there anything we need to do or not do?"

Gretchen chuckles, "I'm fine, we're fine. You are missing the point Malcolm." She waves the ultrasound picture again. "This is a picture of our baby. I know what we are having." She beams.

Malcolm takes the picture from Gretchen's hand. He stares at the grainy image, figures out some features, but not the one that matters for this particular topic of conversation. He heads to the couch; she joins him and takes the picture from him.

"This is obviously the baby's head, and this is the spinal cord, and these two things right here and here are the feet, and if you look closely you can see that our daughter is sucking her thumb."

Malcolm's smile gets so wide his face looks positively painful. "Woman, you've damned near made me the happiest man in the world. A daughter. We're having a girl," he whispers against her smiling cheek.

78 has a new name.

Granger Mitchell and Curtis Morgan greet one another as the 'long-time-no-see' friends they are. They spend a few minutes introducing their wives and remarking on how curious the current circumstances are. When Malcolm, Gretchen, and Bertha pull onto the driveway, all conversation stops. Curtis kisses his wife's cheek then approaches the car. He opens the back door and offers his hand to Bertha King Price. She accepts it. When her feet find ground, Curtis wraps her into his arms, "Bertha you did a fine job raising our son. I knew way-back-when you were too good for me—you went and proved me right."

Tears threaten Bertha's eyes, "I sure did. Now unhand me, and introduce me to your wife. Our son says you did right fine for yourself."

Madison Carlisle Morgan joins Curtis and Bertha. She wraps her arms around her predecessor and whispers, "Thank you for loving Curtis deeply. He owes much to you, Bertha."

The proudful woman leaves the warm embrace, "My appreciation for that Mrs. Morgan, but I suspect **you've** made this man."

The women take hands and nod their heads knowingly.

Gretchen and Malcolm have remained in the Land Rover watching the scene unfold. When Bertha and Madison clasp hands, he steps out and joins them and proclaims, "There's a deep understanding why Curtis Morgan chose you two women to love," he kisses each on the cheek then turns to open Gretchen's door. She is beaming when she exits the car. She extends her hand to Madison Morgan who immediately pulls her close, "Handshakes are for business deals, hugs are for family."

Gretchen spins to Mama Girl, "You said those exact words the day I first met you."

Mama Girl nods, "True words, Gretchen— they're the only kind worth their salt."

That day, the assembled family members discussed the situations at hand and strategized how best to release the information to the public. After concerns and comments were made, Madison spoke—all others listened.

"Curtis, you should make the paternity announcement by yourself. Make a statement— do not take questions. Immediately following the presser, you and Malcolm should sit for an interview, here at Moon River, with the top reporter from each of the top two newspapers. Bertha, Gretchen, and I will be present at the meeting. The private setting will be favorable to Bertha when questions arise. She and I will be together during the interview taking away any question about where we stand with one another. With Gretchen in attendance, we will be sending the message that Mr. and Mrs. Curtis Morgan, Ms. Bertha King Price, and Mr. and Mrs. Granger Mitchell, are blending their families in great anticipation of their grandbaby."

Early evening is spent getting to know one another and sharing stories from the past. There are many mentions of the curious nature of life and of the joyous event that will soon bond the families. Early evening, when everyone is gathered in the great room, Gretchen and Malcolm stand near a magnificent fieldstone fireplace. Gretchen places one hand on her baby bump, and the other into Malcolm's hand. He strokes his thumb over her knuckles in gentle agreement of the moment. "Malcolm and I learned the gender of 78 and we would like to share the news."

Anticipation abounds.

Gretchen squeezes Malcolm's hand, "May I speak with you privately?"

He nods and moves away with her. She takes both of his hands in hers, "When I learned we were expecting, a girl's name came to me in a dream. It has danced through my thoughts so often that I've suspected for some time that we are having a baby girl. I've been calling our little one by this name for weeks."

Malcolm nods and places his hand on her belly bump, "What's the name of our girl?"

Gretchen smiles wide, "My mother's name was Delaney Rae. I want to name our girl, DelRae."

Malcolm nods, "DelRae. It's beautiful. And will our daughter have a middle name?"

Gretchen squinches her face, "Well, after seeing that Curtis is a product of the love of Bertha and Madison, I'm thinking we should affirm the love you had for Sage. So, if it's all the same to you, I think our girl should be named DelRae Finley Price."

Malcolm nods, "I think that is a fine name you have chosen."

Gretchen pulls her man back into the great room and immediately announces, "We are having a girl, and her name is DelRae Finley Price."

Happiness abounds.

Sunday
Morning

Penny

"Pay dirt," Penny whispers. She is staring at a photograph that ran in an early 1980s edition of Savannah's *Daily Morning News*. She knows in an instant that she is looking at the parents of Malcolm Price. She pushes from her desk and races through the newsroom to get to the super-sleuth, a computer system with search capabilities beyond what her desktop system has. Penny works feverishly at the behemoth, and in a matter of a few hours she has the story that will make her the envy of her profession.

Senator Curtis Morgan is
the father of Malcolm Price.

The excited, yet petrified, reporter picks up the phone and makes a predawn call. Twenty minutes later, her editor, Keefer Geist, storms into the newsroom, "My office, now."

Penny grabs her work and scurries inside the ass-reamer's office. "Explain," he demands.

"I'm willing to stake my career, if I still have one after this meeting, that Senator Curtis Robert Morgan is the father of Malcolm Price."

The editor glares.

She stammers on, "The fact that no one knows who Price's daddy is started bothering me, and my nose started twitching, which usually means there's a less than favorable story just below the radar. Anyway, I used the paper's systems after hours to start digging and I found this," she hands off the picture that was taken at the fountain at Forsyth Park in Savannah, Georgia. "The girl in the photo is Bertha King Price, and you know the young man as the current Senator Curtis Robert Morgan of Georgia."

Keefer Geist examines the photograph, "Continue."

Penny gives him printed documentation that confirms Curtis Morgan's return to Georgia after graduating Yale Law school in 1981. "He rented a small apartment near the Historic District in Savannah, passed the Georgia Bar exam, and became an attorney at the Chatham County District Attorney's office in 1982. That places him in the city where that fountain is located during the time it was taken. This documentation confirms the residence of Bertha King Price from that same time. She lived at the Sackville slums and was enrolled at the local high school until shortly after the New Year of 1982. Seventeen-year-old Bertha showed up in Lewisburg some time that month and her son— I believe Malcolm Price is **their** son—was born seven months later."

Geist paces his office. As he paces, he reads and rereads the documentation. He plants himself in front of his corner to corner windows and speaks over his shoulder, "Find out how Bertha Price supported herself during that time, and see if there is anything to indicate Morgan knew about his kid, or that **he** supported it. Not a word to anyone, Penny."

The plucky reporter spends most of Sunday morning running leads and seeking input from her boss. They have found nothing to indicate Senator Morgan knew about his son or provided any financial assistance to him. What Penny did find is much more interesting and damaging to the Malcolm Price family. She beelines to her boss, "Bertha King Price may have supported herself by working for The Bus Company a popular girl-for-hire organization in the 1980s. **This** is the bombshell."

Sunday
Morning

Abigail

The woman who wants answers and who has decided to do a little revenge-seeking of her own spends the early part of her day sipping Kahlua and milk, and part of her mid-morning doing shots of Café Patron. During both timeslots Abigail makes unhinged phone calls that go unanswered and unreturned. Her intended recipients of those calls: Penny Meehan and Senator Turner Rodgers.

Sunday
Afternoon

Penny

The reporter and editor are in deep conversation about the call girl when there comes a shout from the newsroom, "Senator Curtis Morgan of Georgia is about to hold a press conference."

Keefer Geist knows what the senator is about to announce at that presser. "*Liberty Rings* is about to be scooped by the senator, himself." Geist points to his office door, "Meehan you're fired, get your ass out of my office, and out of this building. You have three minutes."

Sunday
Afternoon

Curtis Robert Morgan
Malcolm Price

The senator walks to a bank of microphones that are set up on the driveway of his waterfront estate. "Good morning. I have an announcement of a personal nature to make. I will not be taking questions. In 1981, I had a loving relationship with Bertha King Price. She is the mother of my son, Malcolm Price. Most of you know Malcolm as 77, former point guard of the San Antonio Spurs."

A hushed-tone rumbling begins.

"It wasn't until Malcolm went pro in 2003 that I learned of his existence. It wasn't until this week that he and I met for the first time."

The senator is interrupted by a chorus of chirping cell phones, "I see your newsrooms have done some research already. When you answer those calls you will learn that Ms. Price is considerably younger than I."

A shout comes from the presser, "Eleven years younger, Senator. At the time of your relationship, Ms. Price was seventeen to your twenty-eight. That age difference was, and still is, illegal in the state of Georgia. Care to comment, Senator?"

Curtis nods. "I ignored the laws of the great state of Georgia in favor of the laws of my heart."

"Why did Ms. Price leave you when she became pregnant, and why did she keep your son secret from you for all of these years?"

"Because of the laws of the great state of Georgia. Thank you for coming today."

The senator leaves the gaggle and heads inside his home where he meets a waiting Malcolm. The father and son embrace, then escort a reporter from the New York Times, and another from the Washington Post, to the senator's home office a short distance from the main house. Bertha King Price, Madison Morgan, and Gretchen Mitchell are awaiting their arrival. The reporters get the senator and the mayoral candidate on the record confirming the paternity issue, then they turn their questions to the only person from whom they want to hear.

"Ms. Price, did you leave the senator because of the unlawful acts he committed?"

"We committed. What Curtis and I had behind closed doors was far from unlawful, though we knew if people found out about us they would only focus on our age difference. Seems not much has changed in nearly forty-years."

"Ms. Price, you raised your son in the projects in Lewisburg while on government assistance, yet you purchased a small row house when Mr. Price was in high school. There is no record of your employment, how did you earn the money to buy that house?"

Madison takes hold of Bertha's hand a second before she answers, "I was an escort-for-hire."

"You mean you were a hooker, a prostitute?"

Malcolm shifts his position against the far wall and addresses the reporter, "Show respect, or I'll be showing you the door."

Bertha raises her hand to silence your son. "Yes, young man, I was a prostitute."

The reporter addresses his next question to Malcolm, "When did you first learn what your mother did for money?"

Malcolm wants to say he learned about his mother when he was seven years old; that the older boys in the neighborhood told him his mother worked for The Bus Company. He wants to say he cried himself to sleep most nights worrying about whether his Mama Girl would be safe enough to return home. He wants to say that when his wife worried herself about telling him—he already knew.

Bertha waits for Malcolm's answer. A realization dawns that when he came to her home the other night he never asked a single question about her life as a paid sex worker. His **only** interest was his father. Bertha realizes—in that moment—her son has always known how she earned her money.

Bertha nods her head to her boy.

He nods in return, "I was seven when I first learned."

Sunday
Afternoon

Abigail Forrester
and those who mean her harm.

Abigail watches the senator's news conference live, then on a continuous loop from the comfort of her living room. Each replay brings Abigail closer and closer to her breaking point. When it comes to pass, she picks up a lamp and throws it through her front window. The fired up redhead stumble-storms outside, steps over broken glass, and retrieves her lamp. She is stumbling back to her condo when Penny Meehan stalks toward her.

"You fucking bitch! I knew I shouldn't have thrown in with you. I told you what I would do if I got fucked because of this story! You better get your ass the fuck back inside Abigail, because I have a deep need to fucking beat your brains in."

Abigail pushes past Penny. "Get out of my way," she slurs. Before she closes the condo's front door, she warns, "Get off my property or I'm calling the cops."

Benton Brettenvue watches Senator Morgan's news conference from the treadmill in his downtown Philly office. The huffing and puffing man *is not* huffing and puffing because of physical exertion. Rather, he can't pull an adequate breath because he is laughing his ass off. "Got to give it to you, Abigail, there was dirt to be found on Malcolm Price and his mother. The problem is, you didn't find it in time, and your nemesis bested you once again. Current score: Price 2, Forrester 0."

Senator Turner Rodgers is toasting his good fortune in a dimly lit, oak paneled, brick fireplaced den in his stately home in Alexandria, Virginia. "What a fortuitous turn of events. The Democratic candidate most likely to run against me in the general election just blew his political aspirations to smithereens. And if by some chance the opposing party is stupid enough to back Curtis Morgan for President, then at least the playing field has been leveled." Rodgers pulls a long sip of gin from an oversized tumbler and thinks about giving Abigail Forrester a call. After all, the manipulative bitch has been trying to reach him for days.

Damn frizzy redheaded nemesis.

Malcolm goes directly to the campaign office when he returns to 275. He finds Researcher Randy and the new girl in a rather steamy moment.

He turns to leave when Randy calls out to him, "Batman returns."

"I am not Batman," Malcolm growls.

"You sure sound like him," the new girl says on a giggle. She walks to Malcolm and extends her hand, "I'm Peyton."

"The future Supreme Court Justice. I've heard some things about you. It's a pleasure, Peyton," he shakes her hand. He turns to Randy, "I have a research project for you on consolidations and mergers."

Peyton chimes in, "Interesting topic, I did a term paper on it at UPenn."

"You're being promoted, Peyton, I'd like you to work with Randy on this. Wait here." Malcolm calls out to Gretchen, who is currently face down on the game room couch. "Are you up for a discussion on consolidations and mergers?"

She pushes up, she sits up, she stands up on a growl, "Sure, why not, consolidations and mergers is wonderful small talk," she quips, then enters the office on a sneeze and a cough.

Malcolm laughs at the chirpy sound, "You okay, Woman?"

She nods.

He lifts his hand to her forehead, "You're warm. You and 78 are going to bed, right after this."

"This?"

"Peyton did a research paper at UPenn on consolidations and mergers, and she is about to share a bit of what she knows."

"I'll make it quick, Mrs. Adjacent," Peyton smiles. "In Pennsylvania, municipalities are incorporated territories governed locally, and classified as cities, counties, boroughs, and townships. The process of consolidation, in basic terms, is when municipalities come together to form a new municipality, which in turn forms a new government. The major stipulation to consolidation is that municipalities must be contiguous."

Gretchen tosses a question, "So, using Union County as an example, since all of the municipalities are contiguous they could consolidate, disband their original governments and form a new government?"

Peyton affirms. "Yes, in theory more so than in practice. The problem with consolidation is that even though municipalities may be contiguous, they may also be very different from one another. For example, my farming community doesn't need what your trendy urban community needs, so these two municipalities are unlikely candidates for consolidation. But it's very possible for consolidation to take place if citizens are conned or government officials are squeezed. If some shyster makes a move toward consolidation, things will get very dicey for residents living in those communities. For example, if a consolidation process brings more farming communities into the new government structure than it does trendy urban communities, only one subset of the voting block will be represented in the way they want to be. In this case, the farmers would benefit from the consolidation."

Peyton receives knowing nods all around, so she continues. "Mergers on the other hand are what they sound like, and the process is less complicated. Essentially, one municipality takes over another municipality—the one doing the taking keeps their government in power."

Randy jumps in, "So, if someone like Topher Griffin has a desire to expand freaking fracking across the state of Pennsylvania, and he became mayor then governor, he could manipulate communities — maybe consolidate a few here and merge a few there, and frack the whole damned Commonwealth?"

"Not as mayor of Lewisburg," Gretchen tosses in.

"But as governor of Pennsylvania," Malcolm tosses in.

Peyton nods. "Absolutely. Griffin could make banging bucks from it, too. Let's use the farming municipalities as an example. Fracking requires land. If a bunch of land rich communities consolidate, and the new government sneaks in the backdoor with a plan to frack the shit out of the land, it won't matter if the residents want to keep their land for farming – it will be used for fracking. Keep in mind consolidation isn't easy. So far there hasn't been a successful consolidation of more than two contiguous municipalities in Pennsylvania. This is partly attributed to a 1975 piece of legislation that requires all consolidation plans go through a referendum procedure that gives the voter at least some control over what happens. Still, someone with time, balls, and ingenuity could run a few consolidation games and come out a winner."

"Someone like Abigail Forrester," Malcolm suggests.

"Damn frizzy redheaded nemesis," Randy sneers.

1-2-3-4-5

Abigail is as drunk as she has ever been and nearly passed out when the phone calls start coming in after midnight.

"What do you want Turner?" she slurs.

"To press your bruise for a while. There's no way the news about Senator Morgan being the father of Malcolm Price will hurt the young candidate. Hell, that young black man could run for any office he damn well wants and win it— even Governor of the Commonwealth of Pennsylvania. Admit it Abigail, Griffin can't win. You just lost mayor, which means you just lost governor in 2022." He stops talking and starts laughing. "Best of all, you just lost the damn consolidation and merger tower you've been working on for the last twenty years."

"Fuck you, Turner. As a matter of fact, I may just fuck you out of your run for President," Abigail threatens before hanging up.

Abigail answers the next call thinking it is Turner, again. "Fuck you," she screams, then angers further when she hears Benton's laugh. "What do you want Benton?"

"To let you know that I'm hard and getting harder by the minute, thinking about how far you've fallen. How does it feel being buried beneath that damn block tower of yours? You're washed up, Abigail. Take whatever comfort you can from knowing you're going out in spectacular fashion, undone by the dead whore lover and living whore mother of Malcolm Price."

"Fuck you, Benton. As a matter of fact, I may just fuck you and that plastic bitch wife of yours with a little information drop to the FBI," Abigail threatens before hanging up.

Abigail lets the call from Topher Griffin go to voicemail, then listens. "If you haven't seen the spike in polls for Malcolm Price, then you suck at your job. Wait, you've already established you suck at your job. Come to think of it, you no longer have a job. You're fired. I'm withdrawing from the mayoral race tomorrow. That leaves me with time on my hands. You know what they say about idle hands being the Devil's workshop. Hope you enjoy Hell, Abigail."

Abigail shuts off her cell phone after the call from Penny Meehan, the one where the reporter threatens to bludgeon the fucking redheaded bitch with a shovel then bury her six feet deep.

The call from Mayor Jack Cane goes directly to voicemail.

When mid-morning light assaults the hell out of her, the barely functioning woman, drags her ass up, stumbles to the bathroom, splashes very cold water onto her very puffy face, and throws back a handful of OTC pills that are guaranteed to stop a pounding headache. "We'll see," she mocks as she bumps along the hallway toward the top of the stairs. She changes direction, then pauses when she opens her office door. The disturbance lifts tiny dust particles that filter through blinding sunlight and land on filing cabinets that line the walls of the office. She scoffs at the sight of them, "Every damn governmental structure, of every damn city, county, borough, and township in the damn state of Pennsylvania are in those fucking cabinets, along with the names of every politician on the take. It's all a fucking wasteland now." She walks to her desk, thinks about toppling her Tower of Power, then thinks better of it. "I may have lost the governor's office in 2022; I may not be able to play with ALL of my blocks, but there's ONE block that I can play with—the very first block I laid!"

The vengeful woman closes the office door behind her and heads to the stairs muttering along the way, "Looks as though it's time for a new hobby." With each step Abigail Forrester takes, she mentally packs away her blocks and begins shuffling a deck of cards for her new game of…

WAR

Busted lips and barracudas.

Celia Brettenvue cowers in her walk-in closet waiting for the purring sound of Benton's BMW pulling from the driveway. She has been on the closet floor since the middle of the night...

Benton Brettenvue was stone cold sober, pissed beyond measure, and horny as hell when Abigail Forrester disconnected from his call. He remained on the line—waiting for the **other** woman to disconnect from that same call. "Celia," he smirked at the sound of the phone's click, "eavesdropping again?" He grabbed hold of his hard, pulsating dick, "Well, you need to be punished for that."

Benton stormed down the hall and kicked his wife's bedroom door practically from its hinges, "Spread your damn legs, or I'll spread them for you."

"Get out, Benton. Find another whore to replace Abigail, or take matters into your own hand, but don't you take one more step toward me!" Celia screamed.

He stormed the rest of the way, grabbed her hand before she made it off her bed, threw her onto her back, ripped off her panties, and pushed in. He ignored her struggle, her threats, her pleas, her cries of pain.

As he tucked the ramrod he used as punishment back into his pants, he stood at the foot of her bed. "I will fuck you whenever I want. As long as I'm able to keep you out of prison, consider me your fucking warden. Leave the goddamn door unlocked from now on."

Celia had no sooner returned to bed having tended herself in a warm bath when he made his appearance at her heavily damaged bedroom door. He repeated his previous words, "Spread your damn legs, or I'll spread them for you."

Her next round of words were different from her previous ones, "Benton, I can't...you've...please don't."

His hand tore across her face and opened a gash on her lip. He mounted her and pushed in, and in, and in. When he was done he kissed her hard, licking and pushing against her cut lip, tasting her blood. "Get some sleep. I won't be back tonight."

From the door he called to her, "I haven't tasted your blood in a long time, Celia. I might just come back again later."

The cowering, battered, woman is covered in bruises and is ripped to hell inside from the back to back rapes. She thought about sneaking to the panic room in the den during the wee hours, but she would have had to pass Benton's room, so she stayed on the closet floor praying he wouldn't return.

She pulls herself onto shaky legs when she hears the Alpina leave. She waits an extra minute before heading to the bathroom where she allows herself a good cry and gives herself a good scolding. "You are getting what you deserve, Celia. You took to the Devil's bed to amass a fortune, to be envied, to wield power. You turned a blind eye and a deaf ear to your own daughter and the things she endured." She diverts her eyes from her battered image and takes in the splendor around her, "A magnificent en suite bath, off of a spacious bedroom, inside a palatial house — a house of cards," she sneers. "If I pull one, just one, the whole fucking house will fall."

Celia Brettenvue reaches a trembling hand toward the medicine cabinet, grabs a couple of OTC pills, swallows them with water she drinks from a crystal tumbler, and heads to the shower. "I need to pull that fucking card, so I can put an end to this fucking nightmare."

Mitchell and Morgan

Granger and Faye Mitchell enter the executive suite a bit later than usual to find a broken and beaten Celia Brettenvue waiting for them. Faye goes to the woman and gently helps her from the chair and supports her weight as they make their way into Granger's office. For the next few minutes, the husband and wife attend to the battered woman.

When she is ready, she speaks, "I need all of this to be over, Granger. I know there is prison time in my future, but I'll take comfort knowing I won't be the only one behind bars. I need your advice as to how to approach the authorities. I need someone to accompany me to my bank in Drexel Hill. And I need a safe place to stay. I cannot return to my home. If I do, I will most assuredly die there."

Granger addresses Faye, "Please cancel all of my appointments and have McKay Wallace join us as soon as she is able."

McKay Wallace is a brilliant defense attorney, one who works exhaustively to keep her clients **out** of a courtroom. She believes that no matter the outcome of a trial, a lawyer has lost their case the minute it is brought into a courtroom and turned over to jurors and judges. On the rare occasion when McKay finds herself in court, she is the lawyer who is easily distinguishable from all other legal professionals, she will be the one in a wrap-dress and pair of pumps. The legal strategist does not wear, or even own, the ubiquitous uniform of the female attorney – a pencil-skirt and fitted blazer. McKay's fashion is soft; it does not suggest she is a barracuda. When she opens her mouth, however, any preconceived notion of her is quashed when she begins her verbal laceration of witnesses—as is expected of any self-respecting barracuda.

There is one other thing about McKay Wallace that sets her apart from everyone else at the firm; she does not mince words. She looks at Celia and proves that point, "I hope you punched back. If not, let's get you ready, so you can deliver your own ass-whooping to whoever beat the shit out of you."

McKay turns to Faye, "Would you get me a couple of OTC pills? I feel a headache coming. And get some for her. That busted lip has got to hurt."

5-4-3-2-1

Abigail has been sitting at her kitchen table for two hours, a pen rests on a blank pad of paper next to her cell phone. She is eager to wage WAR, but she is having difficulty choosing her first casualty. She's scrolled through the incoming calls from the night before at least a dozen times. The frustrated warrior picks up her pen and hovers it over the pad just as a thought moves through, *Follow the phone calls*. She writes the names in the order in which the calls came: Turner Rodgers, Benton Brettenvue, Topher Griffin, Penny Meehan. She immediately draws a line through the reporter's name, "You're out on your ass from the paper, so you're not worth my effort." She adds Jack Cane to the list, "Payback for that two-minute voicemail of you laughing. Let's see who's laughing when I'm done with you, Mr. Kinky Pants."

Abigail reviews the list—she adds one more name.

5

Jack Cane searches for his cell phone – he finds it in his wife's hand.

"You called her!? What is wrong with you, Jack? We were free and clear of Abigail Forrester. She'd left you in the dust and found other people to torment, but you just couldn't let the dust settle, could you? NO! You had to go whip it all up, again," Monica Cane screams and paces through their beautiful home set on a beautiful parcel of historic land.

The mayor says nothing, does nothing.

"That's right, Jack, just stand there. We both know I'll be the one to handle this fuck up. Like all of the others. The problem here, Jack, is that this fuck up won't go away easily."

Someone needs to kill a bitch.

4

Topher Griffin arrives for his press conference, surprised that anyone even showed. The usually, 'take it as it comes' Topher, suffers through question after agonizing question.

"Have you seen the polls? ... What is it, a 40 point swing in the overnight polls? ... Hey, where is your campaign manager? ... Shouldn't she be here in a show of support? Did you fire her? Did she quit? Are you two still on speaking terms?"

Topher walks from the borough office through Hufnagle Park to his campaign office.

When he gets inside, he locks the door behind him, picks up an office chair and hurls it through Abigail's fishbowl office window.

Someone needs to torch that witch.

3

Penny Meehan's face displays a whole range of emotion on behalf of Topher Griffin. "Damn! This is brutal and unnecessarily long. He should just walk away. Walk away!" When the cameras pull back she gets a glimpse of reporters from *Liberty Rings*. "I would have been there. I should be there. If not for that redheaded piece of shit. That fucking bitch killed my career. Well you know what they say, payback's a bitch."

Someone needs to dig a ditch.

2

Benton Brettenvue is pacing his office. Abigail's threat about calling the FBI is banging a torturous beat through his head. He **knows** Abigail would fuck him over in a heartbeat, but in doing so she knows she'd be taking on Antonio Alvarez. "She's smart. She has to know that flipping on me will unleash the wrath of the fucking Peruvian. And she knows there's someone powerful enough to keep Roland Gaffney from turning on The Realm associates." Benton exhales a sigh of relief before doubts creep back in, "She wouldn't dare turn me in to the Feds—would she?"

Someone needs to kill a snitch.

1

Senator Turner Rodgers is nursing a gin fueled headache and chastising himself for poking the bear. "You shouldn't have called her. Damn sure shouldn't have pushed her bruise and pissed her off. Now you've got her threat hanging over you." The GOP Presidential candidate throws an empty tumbler against the wall of his study and rails against his stupidity. "Fuck it all! Abigail Forrester doesn't just talk about retribution, she will make sure she gets it."

Someone is going to hire a goddamn hitman.

Project Frizzball

Gretchen hears voices coming from the kitchen and heads there on a cough and a sneeze. She finds Randy, Peyton, and Malcolm getting ready for lunch. Malcolm walks to his woman and kisses her.

Randy shakes his head at the display of affection. "That's some love for sure, Mrs. Adjacent, cuz you aren't looking your best."

Malcolm and Peyton share a laugh.

Gretchen scowls.

"You any better, Woman?" the husband asks as he touches her bump and her forehead.

"No. What's going on?"

"The Kid and The Justice are about to fill me in on their research project," Malcolm smiles.

"Project Frizzball is officially under way," Randy announces.

"Let me grab a shower, I want to hear this. And Malcolm, don't join me," she calls over her shoulder.

"Wasted words, Woman."

Randy and Peyton share a laugh.

The man who wants to be mayor and the woman who wants to breathe freely through her nose are on the game room couch. Her head rests on a pillow on his lap; his fingers are running through her newly cropped hair. Her eyes close on and off. "Are you purring?" he asks on a laugh.

Gretchen sniffles, "Drowning."

Malcolm addresses Randy and Peyton, "You ready, because we're losing her?"

"Just flipping a coin for the jump ball, 77." The Kid wins and begins. "I did some deep diving on Abigail Forrester. Unfortunately, I couldn't swim in her financials because my flippers are constrained by that one," Randy points at Malcolm. "I placed a call to the Decadent One at RFI." Randy waits for the Batman growl, he gets it. "I know, I know, I'm only supposed to contact RFI cyber huntress #3 in an emergency, but the frizzy redhead is a def con scale emergency in my book."

Malcolm nods.

Randy continues, "I wanted a travel history for the redheaded nemesis, beginning in 2003, the year she graduated Georgetown and left DC. The list is long—meaning the number of red frizzballs scattered across the damned state are alarming."

Gretchen sniffles a laugh.

Malcolm is fighting his.

Randy points to Peyton, "You're up Madam Justice."

"I love it when you call me that," she stretches her bow lips into a tiny smile. "Okay, here's some important stuff. The frizzball's trudging began in the coal region of northeastern Pennsylvania where diehard miners hold tight to the struggling anthracite industry and where municipalities are ripe for consolidations and mergers. From there she bounced between the northwestern and southwestern part of the state. She spent copious amounts of time in these areas. I think Abigail is going to execute a consolidation/merger plan, and it has three prongs to it.

First prong: consolidate municipalities in northeastern PA, then choke the life out of the coal mining industry. Second prong: expand the fracking that's already being done in the western part of the state at the Marcellus Shale, and go south and deep into the Utica Shale, a mega-rich natural gas resource. Third prong: get a lacky in as governor to mitigate fracking-related regulations and taxes. Whatever the frizzball's ultimate freaking fracking goal is, she will need someone at the helm of Pennsylvania to deal with existing fracking roadblocks and those that will come down the pike when people start putting two and two together."

Peyton waves her arm toward Randy, "Bring it home, Kid."

"The frizzball and the former mayoral candidate must be fuming that they got fracked out of the fucking race because without the mayorship, there is no governorship, and their freaking fracking ship is sunk," Randy finishes.

"Yeah, and if the frizzball can't move forward on consolidation and mergers she'll be looking for a way to parlay her dastardly designs," Peyton finishes. "We're placing bets she's gonna go after the presidential race." The Kid and The Justice take a finishing bow at the waist.

Gretchen's laughter is caught up in a whole lot of coughing.

Malcolm smiles big, "Glad you two are on my team."

Gretchen and Peyton head to the kitchen. Along the way, the young woman broaches a subject, "Mrs. Adjacent, do you know anything about The Kid?"

"In what respect," Gretchen asks, suddenly aware that she doesn't know **anything** about Randy.

Peyton flips that cart and tells Gretchen a thing to two. "Do you know he's a veritable computer genius? That he graduated top in his class from M.I.T. That governmental agencies like FICA, the FBI, and the CIA have been recruiting him for years?"

The stunned woman slumps against a wall near the kitchen. She is still there when the men happen upon her. "Woman, you okay? You sort of look like—I don't even know what you look like," Malcolm quips.

"You look r.e.a.l.l.y. w.h.i.t.e." Randy offers. "Didn't think you could get much whiter than you normally are, but."

Gretchen interrupts The Kid, "I suspect I look astonished, and befuddled, with a little shock thrown in for shits and giggles."

Randy agrees, "You look all that, and bloodless – don't forget bloodless."

Gretchen hooks her finger at Randy, "Come here."

He moves hesitantly toward her.

She inspects him—really inspects him. "Randy, how old are you?"

"Three naught," he smiles, suddenly aware of the happenings.

"You're thirty?" Gretchen stammers.

The Kid smiles, "You can thank genetics for my youthful look. My father is known to get carded from time to time, and he's ancient."

Gretchen turns to Malcolm, puts her hand to a hip that is exceedingly more difficult to locate along her expanding abdomen, and begins a modified word mash, "Malcolm Price, The Justice just informed me that we are in the presence of a veritable computer genius who graduated top in his class from M.I.T. She also informed that Randy is frequently recruited by FICA, the FBI, and the CIA." She looks at Randy again, "Why didn't you ever say anything about this?"

"Why didn't you ever ask?"

Malcolm leans back and shares wall space with his wife. He addresses The Kid, "So, when I told you to have the Decadent One at RFI do deep cyber work for the campaign, you could have done it yourself?"

Randy waves his hand, "Pish, the cyber huntresses are awesome and all, but they'd get the bends if they followed me on one of my dives. Isn't that so, Miss Wells?" He winks at Peyton who manages to stifle a giggle, but fails miserably at stopping her blush.

The gift that keeps on giving.

Penny Meehan makes an early morning call. "Mr. Griffin, this is Penny Meehan, I'm wondering if you are available to meet with me at 10 AM at Hufnagle Park. We have a frizzy redheaded bitch to discuss."

Penny parks her ass on a bench next to a disheveled Topher Griffin. She follows his line of sight through Hufnagle and across 275 Market Street. She recognizes they are sitting directly across from the converted brick factory building that's home to the presumptive next mayor of Lewisburg. "Of all the benches, in all the parks, in all of Lewisburg, you sat on this one?" she does her best Humphrey Bogart imitation.

Topher scoffs, "I'd prefer Rick's gin joint right about now, but you suggested Hufnagle, Penny."

She laughs and nudges, "You can fist some gin, **after** you tell me where Abigail's pile of dirt is. I'm in the mood to unearth her shit, smack her upside the head with my shovel, and bury her six feet deep."

Topher chuckles, "My fantasies are simpler, a roll of duct tape, an accelerant, a book of matches, and the bitch burns."

"I'm not sure if you're serious, Topher, and by all means have at her, but let me make her suffer public humiliation first."

A wide, somewhat sinister smile spreads across the man's face. "She has a master plan involving consolidations and mergers. We were going to decimate the coal industry and turn The Keystone State into the fracking capital of America."

"Tell me more."

"For a couple of decades, Abigail has been fucking her way across the Commonwealth. When she gets dirt on a politician, she puts his name on the bottom of a wooden block and puts the block onto a vertical structure called the Tower of Power."

"A **real** tower of blocks?"

Topher smiles.

Penny searches her memory, "I've been to Abigail's condo, I never saw any wooden tower."

"She keeps it upstairs in her home office."

"You **saw** the Tower of Power?"

He smiles W.I.D.E.

The reporter plays a hunch, "Topher, you know something about the blocks, something big," she sort of asks, sort of declares.

"Abigail boasted that Turner Rodgers was her first block."

"Pay dirt!"

Topher puts his hand onto her thigh to keep her from shooting skyward, "You know,

Penny, she could be lying about Senator Rodgers."

"We'll see."

As soon as Topher leaves the park, Penny places a call to her former boss at the tabloid, *Kiss and Tell*. "I have a story on a DC power player. A sitting senator. I'll give the tabloid first run on my freelance piece."

"What do you want in return?"

"Desk space, use of anyone or anything I need to chase the story, and a retainer."

"How much?"

"Ten grand."

"Done."

Penny Meehan is back at her old stomping grounds within the hour. She locks herself inside a conference room and gets to work. She begins by talking herself through her initial findings, then does a little speculating, "Abigail earned the 1999 internship in the congressman's office, fair and square. She definitely had the scholarly chops to get herself to Washington; it's when she got there that things become interesting. The bitch never returned to Scranton after her semester in DC. She went to Georgetown University. That takes bucks. Not many families from Scranton can afford to send their kid to Georgetown. Maybe Abigail had something on Turner Rodgers and it was big enough to get her a full-ride at Georgetown." Penny thinks a bit, then hones in on how Abigail thinks. "If she had the goods on Rodgers, something big enough for her to finagle a very expensive education, then Abigail has the gift that will keep on giving." Penny makes a mental note, *watch Turner Rodgers' campaign for personnel changes*.

DC

A very pissed off and tremendously strained Turner Rodgers slams his cell onto his desk after the fifth call to Abigail Forrester goes straight to voicemail. "Fucking bitch," he growls. He steals a quick look over his shoulder at the visiting man, the one who is staring out the window at the Washington Monument off in the distance. The senator reigns himself in when The Body speaks.

"Your desperation is showing, Turner. You need to keep your emotions in check and your dick in your pants." The man in charge moves from the window, taking a seat opposite the senator. "My plans will not be ruined, Turner. I am in this for the long-haul. You won't be in this much longer if things don't get worked out with Ms. Forrester. The Realm has work to do, and thanks to Dominique Brettenvue, the organization is still operational. We owe her a debt for convincing RFI that the program leaders of our side project, Tango, were the leaders of The Realm. That brilliantly duplicitous move left the Gang of Eight in place and bought us time. I have **no** intention of wasting that time dealing with your fuck ups. Abigail Forrester is a problem. Handle the problem. If you do not, Turner, you will be a problem for me and we all know how I deal with problems."

Philly
Abigail spends all day planning her first battle in her game of WAR, "Turner. Turner. Turner. Do I ruin your chances of becoming President, or do I get you under my thumb?"

No-brainer!

The plotting and planning redhead is in her office when she answers the sixth phone call from the senator, "Starting to sweat, Turner?" Abigail says on a laugh.

"You won't ruin my chances of becoming president."

Her laugh gets more animated, "Oh, really, and why is that?"

"Because you want me in the Oval Office, Abigail."

"And why is that Turner?"

"Power. Mine and yours," he plays his trump card.

Abigail pauses, then pushes. "Make me your campaign manager and then we'll talk about where I want to be in your administration. These are my non-negotiables, Senator."

He knew going into this phone call that those were going to be her non-negotiables. "Be in DC at the end of the month."

"The announcement that I'm your manager, are you going to make it, or will I? I don't much care, but it needs to be done **before** I come to Washington."

"Don't worry, Abigail, everything will be done before you get to DC." The senator disconnects from the call, takes a single use phone from his desk and taps in a phone number. A woman answers with a single word, "Irish."

"Tell Boston I have a problem in Philadelphia that needs to be handled."

"The problem's name?"

"Abigail Forrester."

*Private investigators and
defense attorneys.*

Benton hasn't seen nor heard from his wife in days. She hasn't been home, hasn't returned any of his calls, hasn't made any transactions on their shared bank or credit card accounts. The increasingly agitated man has been pacing his office for hours, an unopened whiskey bottle heavy in his hand. He's resisted the urge to drink, thus far, but he knows it is only a matter of time before he cracks the seal.

The drunk gently sloshes the amber liquid around in his mouth. He savors the hints of leather, wood, and tobacco flavors that skip along his tongue and travel down his throat. "I've missed you," he growls long and low, as the elixir's warmth spreads downward and outward. He becomes hard. He smiles and pulls another sip. This mouthful strengthens his erection and sets off some spewing. He rants to his old friend in a bottle, "Where the fuck is she? Is she with the fucking Feds? Is she giving them the goods on me? Is she in protective custody? She'd better fucking be—if she's snitching."

Benton takes another l.o.n.g. p.u.l.l. He follows the booze to the cold, hard truth, "It's payback time. Celia is going to fuck me all the way to federal prison." The rape scenes from the other night start banging through his head, and a similar rage takes hold. "I didn't even want you, Celia. I wanted Abigail. That redheaded bitch pissed the fuck out of me and I took my rage out on you, and now I've got two fucking bitches who need to be silenced."

He loses his erection.

Benton Brettenvue places a call to his private investigator, "I need you to find my wife, and find out whatever you can about Abigail Forrester. I'm mostly interested in what her plans are. Drop whatever else you're working on. I want this information yesterday," he slurs.

Old Estate Road
Celia Brettenvue is beginning to relax now that she's living inside the Mitchell's guarded neighborhood. It has been days since Granger and Faye settled her in to Gretchen's vacant Carriage House with a warning from Attorney Mitchell...

"I am confiscating all of your belongings, Celia. You should hold my next words as firm notice. If you so much as even think about leaving the premises, or contacting anyone outside of my estate, you will be cast asunder to deal with this mess on your own."

She nodded her understanding, even managed to hold her tears until after he'd left.

Celia considers herself very lucky to be living in comfortable captivity, even though the comfort level diminishes greatly when McKay Wallace shows for her daily round of direct examination. In response to her attorney's directive, Celia spends her alone time making a list of every occasion that she and/or Benton walked up to, stepped onto, or crossed over the legal line.

McKay uses that list to drill down for answers, "Tell me about the SEC violation involving Nixon Petroleum. Who originally bought the stock … who delivered the tip that you and Benton should sell your shares … when was it traded … by whom … what was the financial gain?"

While Celia talks, McKay follows along on a legal pad. When she has questions, she asks them, when she needs a deeper explanation, she drills for it. At such time that the attorney is satisfied they have exhausted a subject, they move on. The only occasion that McKay did not drill for answers was when she read Celia's notation on list #4.

Pimped Dominique out at age seventeen
to Antonio Alvarez.

"You or Benton?"

"Benton arranged it, but I didn't stop it."

McKay put that topic aside. "I need to discuss this with Granger." When the defense attorney arrived for her next session, she brought along the senior partner. Celia immediately knew what was in store.

"Tell us everything you know about your husband and Antonio Alvarez," Granger held her stare, "tell us **everything**, Celia."

She began shaking and choking on her words, "I've been warned not to talk about him." She turned pleading eyes to Granger, "They will kill Dominique if I talk."

The attorney said nothing, yet his countenance spoke volumes.

She silently weighed her predicament and acquiesced. "I met Alvarez about a dozen years ago when Benton brought him to dinner one evening. I have no definitive proof, but I think Benton met him a handful of years before that. It was around that time when our family started falling apart. Until about the age of 10, Dominique had a very wonderful, playful, carefree relationship with her father. They were thick as thieves." She snaps her fingers, "Then just like that, everything changed. Benton began traveling more often with the majority of his trips taking him out of the country. He never called home to talk to Dominique, and when I tried to get hold of him he was unreachable. Around that same time, his circle of business associates changed and his phone conversations became secretive. I started eavesdropping on calls and at the door to his office. That's how I heard the names Antonio Alvarez and Roland Gaffney for the first time. It was also the way in which I heard about The Realm. It was obvious Benton was talking about an organization because he referred to 'the gang of leaders' and a reporting structure. At some point after that, Benton began talking about Tango and linking it to Antonio Alvarez."

"Tell us more about Tango."

"I don't know much, but my understanding is that it is a money-making endeavor."

Granger and McKay excuse themselves for a private discussion, when they return they drop a bomb in Celia's lap.

"We want you and Dominique to talk. If this case continues along the path it's heading, we might not wait for the authorities to come looking for you. We might reach out to them." She begins shaking her head back and forth and wringing her hands. Nervous, hitched breaths settle into her words, "I don't think…"

Granger turns his back on her and walks to the door, "We aren't interested in your opinion, Celia, we are informing you of our strategy. If you don't want to end up living at

LewPen with your daughter, you will prepare yourself for a visit there."

"When?"

"Within the next two weeks."

A busy two weeks.

Two weeks have come and gone since Benton Brettenvue put his private investigator to work. The PI calls and delivers information that is bound to set his employer off.

"On the day Mrs. Brettenvue left the home you two shared, she drove to the law offices of Mitchell and Morgan. She parked her Mercedes at the law firm's underground garage where it has remained ever since. She was witnessed entering the building and arriving at the executive floor. Several hours later, she was driven away from the law firm by Granger and Faye Mitchell. They took her to a bank in Drexel Hill where she spent time inside the bank's vault. She emptied a safety deposit box, drained a bank account, and cancelled her association with the bank before getting back into the Mitchell car. Three separate sources say your wife has been staying at the Carriage House on the Mitchell estate since that day. Defense attorney, McKay Wallace, makes daily visits to the Old Estate property. She usually spends two or more hours with Mrs. Brettenvue."

The PI ignores the shatter of glass coming over the phone line.

"What about the fucking redhead?"

"Ms. Forrester has been keeping a very low profile. She leaves her condo to run errands and to get take out dinners. Other than that, things have been quiet. She's had no visitors, although there's someone else watching her place."

"Who?"

"A guy in a blue Jag."

"Find out who the guy is and what he wants."

The PI disconnects without another word.

Two weeks have passed since Penny Meehan began sifting through Abigail's dirt. She's found plenty of easily proven salacious activity and an abundance of inuendo linking Abigail to some of the biggest movers and shakers in PA and DC, including the heaviest hitter of all—the soon-to-be GOP general election candidate, Turner Rodgers.

Even from her perch in Lewisburg, Penny has tapped into the DC rumor mill. She calls Topher. "Thanks for the lead. It's rumored Senator Rodgers is set to name the bitchy redhead as manager of his presidential campaign. I know Abigail started that rumor, but it's got legs. I need to get to DC before someone scoops me on the bitch and the senator. Be back in touch."

Two weeks have passed since Abigail Forrester fell into a pile of shit that is really a fertilized bed of roses. Just knowing she is parlaying her failures in the Commonwealth of Pennsylvania into a job at the highest levels in DC whips Topher Griffin into a fury. "I need a plan—one with deadly consequences." He readjusts his murder fantasy of burning the witch's house to the ground to a more up close and personal demise. "You need to die at the hands of someone you ruined."

Two weeks have passed since Senator Rodgers hired a contract killer. During that time, the paid assassin known as Boston, has been tailing Abigail Forrester. So far, he knows she owns the two-family, side by side condo unit in a very nice, quiet residential area of Philly; that she lives on one side of the building and the other side is currently vacant; what her daily and nightly routines are; and she has an outdoor mounted security keypad. "Might as well not have bothered with that level of security, Ms. Forrester." Boston checks his watch then spends a few seconds going over his plans. "I've got your code, but it won't be needed if Plan A goes accordingly. If not, I'll definitely need it and your house keys for Plan B. I should have them by the end of the day," he says as he exits his car. He approaches the unsuspecting woman as she is coming out of her condo for her daily run to the takeout joint 3.2 miles from her place.

"Excuse me, Ms. Forrester..." he intentionally startles her. "I'm sorry, I didn't mean to startle you. My name is Paul Boston. I work for Senator Rodgers."

She raises her hand to shade her eyes from the lowering sun, suddenly very happy she did. *Well, hello, Bradley Cooper clone.*

"The senator asked me to meet with you about your relocation to Washington. Do you have a few minutes?" Boston's quick smile shows off a swoon-worthy set of dimples.

Abigail's girls bud to attention and she gets a bit wet down *there* just eyeing the devastatingly handsome man standing on her driveway. The answer she wants to give Mr. Yummy Pants is*, I have all the time in the world.* The answer she actually gives him is, "Yes, of course. The thing is I'm just running to get takeout for dinner. I shouldn't be long," she says through her thin-lipped smile.

"I'd be happy to wait in my car, maybe keep you company while you eat," Mr. Exceedingly Handsome offers.

Abigail nods, a bit too enthusiastically. "Why don't I grab you some takeout, that way I won't have to eat in front of you," she says trying to tamp her excitement.

"I could follow you and we could eat there." Boston tests the waters.

"Actually, I have an appointment with a moving consultant in an hour, so I need to stay close to the condo."

Plan B, he quickly thinks. "In that case why don't you grab me a tuna on rye." Boston hands her a twenty. "Dinner's on me, or should I say, dinner is on the Campaign." Boston dimples, again.

"That's not gonna fly when I'm in charge," she laughs. "I'll be back in fifteen." Boston heads back to wait in his Jag. "Too bad I can't handle you now, but thanks for the info about your appointment with the moving consultant."

The contract killer enjoys dinner with his soon-to-be-victim. "You're from Scranton," he small talks.

Abigail groans, "Don't remind me."

He laughs. "Philly is a better fit for you?"

"It was. I'm looking forward to being in DC again. I've been gone a long time." She pauses—she pushes. "Maybe you'll take me around town, make sure I'm seen at the right places."

He smiles. "Whatever you need to get settled back in. Have you found a place to live?"

"Not yet. I might have to stay in a hotel for a while."

"I'll give you a call tomorrow with a list of realtors who are very plugged in," he offers.

Abigail beams, "Perfect."

Moving consultant, Brenna Campbell, arrives a few minutes early. Abigail escorts the woman in, leaving Boston alone in the kitchen. It's time enough for him to make a wax imprint of her house key. He is standing at the back door looking out over the yard when she returns.

"Paul, I'm sorry, but I have to cut this short."

"No worries. If you need anything call Turner's office, they know how to track me down," he says as he enters the living room and the orbit of Brenna Campbell. He smiles wide at the hippy-chic young woman, then turns to his hostess, "Abigail, it was a pleasure meeting you. I'll be seeing you again."

"Soon," Abigail smiles encouragingly.

"Sooner than you think," Boston winks and dimples.

The women sigh as they watch the man walk away. "He looks like Bradley Cooper," the moving rep sighs.

"Mmmmm," Abigail moans.

Mr. Exceedingly Handsome answers his ringing cell phone as he walks to his Jag. "Boston," he says, turning once more toward the two ogling women.

Chevy Chase
The paid assassin pulls into the garage of his $4 Million, 5-bedroom, 6-bath, stately blonde brick home in Chevy Chase at 7 AM. The sounds of

his life find him when he steps from his Jag. The eager man opens the door that leads from the garage through a mudroom and into an enormous kitchen. A chorus of, "Daddy's home," sings out. He moves backwards in exaggerated form, absorbing the rush of little bodies, flying limbs, and tight-squeeze hugs. "Let's see how many there are today, one, two, three, four," the family man says as he touches each child's head. He moves to his wife, Felicity, who's making breakfast and lunches. "Hey, babe," he smiles wide.

"I need a kiss, then your two oldest need to be encouraged to get dressed for school. Caitlyn will be here to get the twins ready for preschool, and I need to get ready for work."

"Are you in court today?"

His wife laughs. "Nope, in the office all day. You?"

"Working from here, I have a little cleanup from my trip."

Felicity raises a perfectly sculptured brow, "The cleanup. Is it of the normal variety, or did you find problems on your trip?"

"Normal stuff. Just need to tie up a few loose ends and handle some financials. Now, off to work with you, I'll make dinner tonight."

"That's why I married you," Felicity says as she races from the kitchen and up the center staircase.

Paul Ferraro aka Boston is a former Army Ranger who owns a dozen survival training schools across the country called, Intestinal Fortitude. Each school has a primary training focus like desert survival, or deep woods survival, or minimalist survival, or mountain survival, or wilderness awareness. All the training programs are geared for kids and adults, offer a basic survival component, and are booked solid every day of every week of every month of every year for the next three years.

When Boston left the military, he took everything he learned from his Ranger training and direct action and used them to build a successful business. Of course, it's his other business, the one where he gets to kill people, that is booming and beyond financially lucrative.

Wrong place – wrong time?

Well after dark, Benton turns onto Abigail's street; his BMW is instantly caught in a strobe of colorful lights. He is waved to the side of the road by a police officer, "License and registration, please." Benton reaches into his pocket for his wallet, removes his license and opens his glove box for his registration, "Officer, what's going on?"

The officer ignores the question, "You're several miles from home, Mr. Brettenvue, care to explain why you are in this neighborhood?"

"I do not care to explain, Officer."

"Do you know anyone who lives at that address?" The officer points to Abigail's condo.

Benton remains silent.

The officer instructs the driver, "Please step out of your vehicle, Mr. Brettenvue."

I don't think The Realm is dead.

A conference room door opens at the J. Edgar Hoover Building in DC. A formidable woman with skin the color of coal, a close cropped Afro, and burnt-sienna colored eyes, thumps her way to a massive cherry table. Her outstretched hand motions toward two chairs, "Take a seat, gentlemen."

Fred Serpico and Manuel Xavier, lead investigators of the internationally renowned law enforcement agency known as, Rocco Fiancetti Incorporated (RFI), do as they've been instructed.

FICA Director, Stacy Remington, is in command of the room, and she wastes no time, "I don't think The Realm is dead."

The men stiffen and straighten in their chairs.

"The FBI, FICA, and RFI will be working that problem in coming days and weeks." The Director eyes the men to punctuate that the topic is not up for immediate discussion. She slides two case files across the table, "I am turning over the Philadelphia homicide case of Abigail Forrester to RFI. This decision has been approved by the Director of the FBI and the case has been accepted by the head of your organization."

The investigators nod.

"I assume you are able to follow the news at your forested fortress."

The investigators nod.

"Good. The condo where Abigail Forrester lived and died was sealed after the removal of her remains which are at the Philadelphia ME's office waiting to be autopsied at 17:00 hours. Philly Detective, Ted Brothers, took one look around the Forrester condo and concluded the dead woman had connections that went well above the purview of the PPD. He locked down the scene, called the Philly FBI field office, who called FBI Director Webber at J. Edgar. For reasons that will become evident, the investigation landed on my desk. I am handing it off you. Do not fumble this case, gentlemen."

The investigators nod.

The Director continues, "The condo is pristine from an investigative standpoint. Detective Brothers did an observational walk-through, stopped when he saw what the victim had in her home office. I suspect you will find enough dirt in the victim's premises to bury some of the most influential people in America, particularly in the District of Columbia and the Commonwealth of Pennsylvania."

The Director hands two pieces of paper to former FICA Agent Manuel Xavier. "That paper has the phone number for Ted Brothers at the PPD. He has the keys to the condo and will provide reports and observations from his first go-through. He is authorized to coordinate forensics for you. The other paper contains two sets of numbers, the first is a telephone number. The person who answers that phone is the **only** other person outside of RFI with whom you are allowed to discuss your findings—**if** she recites the second set of numbers on that paper, sequentially."

"She?" Fred asks.

"FBI Director, Shelby Webber."

Stacy Remington leaves the conference room without further comment and returns to her office to learn that Granger Mitchell has requested a return phone call. She will return the call from her friend and mentor before she does anything else that day. Seconds into the call she realizes this is not one of pleasure.

"Good morning, Director Remington."

"Attorney Mitchell."

"I believe you may be interested in speaking with Celia Brettenvue. I can arrange that, but it's important the meeting be done away from FBI offices."

"Are you representing Celia Brettenvue?"

"She sought legal representation from my firm several weeks ago and is working with McKay Wallace."

The Director of FICA pauses a moment before addressing the offer. "I'm interested in what Mrs. Brettenvue has to say on certain topics, Granger, however, you and I may be on opposite ends of interest on this one."

"Based on information Celia provided McKay Wallace, and her willingness to provide you information on targets of considerable importance and influence, I believe our interests are aligned."

The FICA Director mulls a bit, "I can be at your office tomorrow at noon."

"We will expect you, Stacy."

Chevy Chase
Boston waits several hours for the wire transfer from Senator Turner Rodgers. It lands in one of Boston's offshore accounts in the Cayman Islands, after having passed through multiple financial institutions across the globe. Boston transfers the $1 Million to another account and closes the Cayman account. By the end of business that day, the paid assassin will have opened another account in the Islands, which will be used for his next assignment. He laughs at his unbelievably good fortune.

Personal? Professional? Both?

An energy pushes against Serpico and Xavier when they enter Abigail Forrester's condo. They push back against it as they move about the first floor, eyeing this, thinking that, processing it all.

Fred is in the kitchen when he calls out to his partner, "Here's the legal pad that alerted Detective Brothers that this homicide needed to be kicked up the chain."

Manuel joins Fred and reads the names on the pad, "Turner Rodgers, Benton Brettenvue, Topher Griffin, Penny Meehan, Jack Cane and .... Curtis Morgan. Well, shit."

"Yeah, shit."

Manuel moves past the familial relationship between Senator Morgan and Malcolm Price and gets back to the task at hand. "Meehan's name is crossed out, and Rodgers' name is circled." Manuel's glove-covered hand lifts a business card from atop the legal pad, "Premium Movers, Brenna Campbell." He puts the card back, leaves the kitchen to Fred for processing and moves to the far corner of the living room where he finds several cardboard boxes. He reads the black marker notations out loud, "Kitchen supplies, linens, winter clothes. The victim was planning a move, for sure.

Maybe the rumors that she landed the gig as Senator Rodgers' campaign manager are based in fact." Manuel moves the first row of boxes forward and finds a big box labeled **Financials** pushed against the wall. He removes the top and fingers through a few files, "Pretty big box for financials. This will take some time to go through."

"Not my wheelhouse," Fred says as he heads upstairs with his partner tight on his heels. They stop at the bedroom door, both feeling the lingering energy of a brutal death. They scan the room from the hallway, then step inside.

"There's evidence of packing," Manuel says. "Things that might be displayed on the top of furniture have been removed and packed into that unsealed box." He moves to a triple-dresser of drawers, of which two are opened. He peeks inside, "The killer probably got the panties he stuffed into her mouth from here."

Fred nods. He's staring at the bare mattress, letting the words Detective Brothers said about the crime scene bang through his head...

"Victim was lying in the center of the bed, pillows were on the floor, one on each side of it, blankets were twisted around the victim's legs and feet, her arms were bent at the elbows, her hands were at shoulder level, her eyes were open, pupils fixed and dilated, and petechial hemorrhaging was noticeable.

There was a piece of duct tape slapped across the victim's mouth, and what appeared to be a piece of silky panty material hanging out one side. When the victim was found, she was wearing a white T-shirt and pair of purple and white silk underwear."

Fred moves to a bedroom window and begins processing. He breaks the silence a few minutes later with the clap of his hands, "The killer is in the house. Let's run the three most likely ways he got inside: he breeched security; he was invited in; he snuck in using a set of keys and the security codes."

"He?" Manuel repeats.

"Just a hunch. The killer is strong and the energy feels sadistically male."

Manuel pushes back, "Could be a woman in the military, or a psycho mercenary like Dominique."

"Since Dominque is in LewPen, we can count her out."

Manuel scoffs, "Never count Dominique Brettenvue out of anything."

Fred nods and gets back to his analysis. "If the killer breeched security there'd be signs of B&E, and the victim and the security provider would have been alerted to an intruder. If a warning were signaled, Abigail would not have been waiting in bed for her killer—unless she was incapacitated somehow. Let's run this as though the killer was in the house because

Abigail invited him in. It's unlikely she would have welcomed a raging man, or woman, into her place, so the killer enters under friendly terms. Abigail was found dead in her bed, and since there's no history of Abigail being sexually involved with women, I'm running this as though the killer is a man. In this scenario, the victim invited a calm, friendly man into her house, and perhaps into her bed. Something happened to make Mr. Calm and Friendly get out of bed, rummage through her panty drawer, take a pair, and stuff it down her throat." Fred takes a look around before continuing, "After stuffing the panties into her mouth, he slaps a piece of duct tape across it." Fred takes another look around.

Manuel pushes in, "None of the boxes are taped shut yet."

"Yeah. Maybe the killer used tape from around here and took it when he left."

"Or brought his own."

"Yeah." Fred thinks a minute then continues, "If this were a crime of passion, the killer wouldn't have taken the time to panty her up and tape her mouth shut. If he's already in bed with her and the mood turns homicidal, why not just roll over and strangle the fuck out of her? Unless he did the whole 'shutting her up' to make a point, then something went wrong and he went too far. Otherwise, it's a bit too labor intensive for it to be a crime of passion. This fits better as a premeditated murder." Fred pauses before beginning again, "Let's run this through the filter that the killer is pissed at Abigail Forrester when he arrives at the condo. If he's raging mad, he isn't going to be invited in, but let's say he gets inside, somehow. He isn't going to take time to rummage through drawers looking for panties and bother with duct tape? He's pissed, he's in the condo, he bashes her head in, or he shoots her, or he stabs her—then he gets the fuck out."

Fred turns and scans the room looking for his partner, "Manuel?"

"In the closet, Fred."

Fred laughs, "You know, I've wondered if you might be gay."

"Fuck you, Fred."

Fred laughs big, "You planning on coming out of the closet?"

"Fuck you, Fred."

Fred laughs a bit more, then gets back to business. "Now let's run this through the filter that the killer had what he needed to get into the condo — a set of keys and the security codes — and he had those because he's a frequent visitor of Abigail's, but he's not a trained killer. If this person wants to kill her, he's most likely going to sneak in, kill her, and get the fuck out, no panties, no duct tape, unless he **wants** her to know she's going to die and that **he** is the one killing her. Maybe he has a few parting words he wants to share; the panties and duct tape would shut her up and give him time to say his piece, but that still makes the killing premeditated."

"And difficult," Closet Man calls out.

Fred looks at the bed again, "The killing feels personal to me, but it feels professional, too. There are a lot of steps involved, more than the average person could handle. It would take a certain skill set to pull off something like this; familiarity with the victim's schedule, access to her keys, knowledge of her security code, the ability to get through the condo undetected, patience, strength, cold detachment, and assuming there are no fingerprints on the duct tape, an understanding of forensics. This has the markings of a contract killing, one where the person who ordered the hit wanted Abigail Forrester to know she was going to die and why she was going to die. The combination of the two explains the personal and professional feel to this homicide."

Fred takes one more long look out the window and finishes his first assessment of the crime scene. "The panties down the throat and the duct tape intrigue me. Using her panties and sealing her mouth shut screams — shut the fuck up you whore!"

Manuel steps out of the closet.

The RFI detectives move down the hall and enter Abigail's home office. They are taken aback by the number of six-foot tall filing cabinets that line the four walls. The only space not dedicated to the vertical metal structures is a section near a window where a desk is placed. On top of the otherwise pristine desktop is a wooden block tower, and sitting next to it is a boxed deck of playing cards.

Fred furrows his brow, "Do you want to pull a block or shuffle the deck?"

"I want to topple the whole damned tower," Manuel laughs.

"We will," Fred assures his partner.

A panic room, a carriage house,
a prison cell.

Stacy Remington thumps into Granger Mitchell's office. The consummate professionals nod their greeting and say nothing more. McKay Wallace hands the director a piece of paper with a written list on it. "Director Remington, we propose you choose three topics from that list and ask one question on each topic. We have instructed our client to keep her answers brief. After the first round of questions, if you want more information from Celia Brettenvue, we will need to discuss the matter of immunity."

Director Remington reads the list and turns toward the door to leave. Granger stops her momentum. "Stacy, the first round is free," he reminds her.

Stacy reviews the list at length, "I don't need Mrs. Brettenvue's help with these matters." She pauses, then plays a longshot, "If your client can give me the name of the operation that Antonio Alvarez and Benton Brettenvue worked on, this meeting may proceed."

Celia waits for nods from both of her lawyers before answering, "Tango," is all she says.

"Let's discuss immunity, Granger." They leave the room without further comment.

The twosome return from their meeting nearly an hour later. The attorney has with him a negotiated agreement, which he shares with the head of his defense department and their client.

"Celia Brettenvue will receive full immunity in return for her cooperation in the Tango and The Realm investigations. She will remain at the Carriage House on Old Estate Road under the protection and supervision of agents assigned to the Federal Bureau of Investigation. She will be required to wear an ankle monitoring bracelet and have limited access to the estate grounds. She will make her herself available to meet with the FBI within 24-hours of an official request. She is allowed to have legal representation with her during all formal questioning. She is allowed to visit Dominique Brettenvue at the U.S. Penitentiary in Lewisburg. Inside the meeting room with her will be her attorneys. She will be given 48-hours' notice if she is to be arrested and will be allowed to turn herself in to the field office in Philadelphia."

Stacy finishes the agreement, "In return, Celia Brettenvue will provide answers to all questions, on any subject presented to her by the Federal Bureau of Investigation. Any noncompliance, incomplete answers, or provable misstatements will render the full immunity agreement null and void." She waits for Celia to ask questions, there are none forthcoming. She waits further as Celia Brettenvue takes the agreement from Granger, signs it, and walks it to the Director of FICA. She hands her the agreement, "You have treated me more fairly than I deserve, Director Remington. Thank you."

Stacy nods, "I hope this works in both our favor, Mrs. Brettenvue." Stacy turns and thumps away.

A Place of Panic

Benton Brettenvue is in the upstairs den of his lavish home busy with preparations for his game of Hide 'n Seek. For the past several hours, he has been dividing his time between stocking his panic room with food, water, and whiskey, and staring through a pair of binoculars at the two access roads that lead onto his property.

"The Feds can't get to me without using those roads, or a helicopter," he scoffs and looks skyward. He takes another look at his sprawling estate, then reluctantly looks at the entranceway to the panic room. The thought of crawling into the tiny space causes his heart to race and a sweat to form from head to toe. He's been in a state of rising panic since he came home from the Philly PD after being questioned about his relationship with the recently departed Abigail Forrester. No matter how hard he tries, the claustrophobic man cannot calm his fears about confinement in small, cramped spaces. He begins pacing the mammoth room in a desperate attempt to distract himself from the Orwellian purgatory that awaits inside the chamber. As he paces, he lets the words of Detective Ted Brothers start banging in his head…

"Mr. Brettenvue, did you have an association with Abigail Forrester?"

"Yes."

"Was the association personal or professional in nature?"

"Both."

"When was the last time you saw Ms. Forrester?"

"I'd have to check my records, Detective, but it was within the last week or so."

"What were the circumstances of that meeting?"

Benton's lawyer placed his hand on Benton's arm as a caution.

The cocky client shook off his lawyer's hand and directed his answer to Detective Brothers. "We ended our affair."

The detective made a few notes on his pad, "Who ended the affair, Mr. Brettenvue?"

Benton's lawyer touched his client's arm again.

He ignored his lawyer's warning, again. "It was a mutual ending to our shagging, Detective. I had no animus toward Ms. Forrester certainly not enough to kill her. Now, if you find my wife dead, you should bring me in for questioning, but as far as Abigail's murder is concerned, you are barking up the wrong tree."

"This is my last question, Mr. Brettenvue. If you and Ms. Forrester ended your affair, why were you on her street the night of her murder?"

The lawyer touched his client's arm.

This time, the client kept his mouth shut.

Benton's thoughts are interrupted by a caravan of black vehicles approaching his estate from both access roads. He steps into the panic room and immediately begins panicking.

A Place of Protection

Granger Mitchell and McKay Wallace get Celia Brettenvue safely back to the Carriage House after her meeting with Director Remington. By early evening, two FBI agents from the Philly field office have introduced themselves, fitted her with an ankle bracelet, and explained the rules, "The permissible range of motion outside the Carriage House is 1,000 feet. That allows you to move about on the back part of the property and get to the back door of the main house, adjacent to this building. An agent needs to escort you whenever you leave the Carriage House. If you step outside without approval, you will be taken into custody. Additionally, if you are not accessible for an FBI visual check, once every 4-hours, you will be taken into custody immediately upon your discovery."

Granger imposes himself into the conversation, "Agents, you will be receiving instructions, if you have not already, that Mrs. Brettenvue will be visiting the U.S. Penitentiary in Lewisburg on Wednesday."

"We are aware, Mr. Mitchell."

"Very well."

"Departure times and protocol are being formalized with the prison, and will be discussed with you at a later date," Crew Cut #1 says.

"Very well," the attorney nods.

A Place of Punishment

The senior partner of the most successful law firm in Philadelphia makes a two-and-a-half-hour drive every Wednesday to LewPen to see Dominique Brettenvue. The visits are under the guise of lawyer-client consultation, but they are really a part of the Granger Mitchell Outreach Program.

The attorney first met with prisoner BOP-PA-555925 when he took over the custody matter between Dominique Brettenvue and Manuel Xavier. When Dominique gave birth to their daughter and Manuel took custody of baby Charlotte, there were no legal reasons for Granger to continue his visits; yet he felt he had a moral reason to do so...

The attorney put a set of legal documents onto the table between them. The prisoner's shackles allowed her to lean forward enough to read the heading.

"Charlotte's adoption is official?" she searched the attorney's face for confirmation.

"Yes."

"Good. Charlotte will be safe with Manuel. Thank you, Granger."

He took the papers and tucked them back inside his briefcase.

Dominique leaned back against the hard plastic chair, "I appreciate your making the trip to show me those papers. I guess this means our business is finished," she said wistfully.

"Well, yes, this legal matter is certified, but you mentioned you wanted to document the criminal activity of your parents. Is that something you are still interested in doing. Before you answer, it would require that you continue meeting with me on Wednesdays."

She offered a small smile. "Yes, Mr. Mitchell, I would like to continue our meetings."

The agenda of those meetings became very unique to this lawyer-client duo. The first fifteen minutes of each session were devoted to the recitation and documentation of the salacious and criminal activities of Mr. and Mrs. Brettenvue. The second fifteen minutes were devoted to warmer memories...

"Things at the Brettenvue homestead weren't all bad, Granger."

"No?"

"No. There was a time when we were all very close, even Celia and me. Every day when I came home from school, I'd sit on the floor of the family den doing homework while Celia sat nearby watching the soap opera, *General Hospital*. I try very hard to block most memories from my childhood, but I actually like this memory and I try really hard to remember the happenings in the fictional Port Charles, New York."

After that disclosure, the larger-than-life Granger Mitchell surprised his client with a reading.

"Is that some sort of publication that tracks the episodes of *General Hospital?*"

He nodded. "Mrs. Granger found it at the drugstore."

Dominique smiled a most beautiful smile that broadened and brightened as her attorney read the little paper book, cover-to-cover.

Those memories are important to the attorney-friend of Dominique Brettenvue. Granger harbors deep concerns that the imprisoned woman will not take kindly to his surprising her with a visit from her mother. He fears she will see this as a betrayal of the relationship he and she have developed. "I sincerely hope this will help my cause, and bring Dominique joy," he reaches into his breast pocket and removes a picture of Charlotte given

to him by Manuel. Granger studies the baby and proclaims, "She favors her mother."

Gentle experimentation.

Malcolm finishes work just before midnight on the eve of the election. He expects to find Gretchen fast asleep having retired hours earlier, so he is surprised to see their bedroom softly lit with candles and filled with the citrusy smell of his woman. He follows the sound of running water to the designated shower room off the master bedroom. It too is aglow with warm flickering light.

Gretchen is leaning against the shower door, her feet crossed at the ankles, a devilish smile on her face, and nothing else on her body. He laughs at her attempt to mimic his familiar stance.

"Woman, are you in need of some gentling?" He asks as he begins stripping.

She nods.

He wraps his arms around her, pulling her gently to him, their baby bump creating a barrier against the closeness they usually share. Malcolm laughs, "Looks like some gentle experimentation is in order." He opens the shower door and follows her inside. The warm, steamy water welcomes and arouses. Malcolm inches toward her until her back is pressed against the shower wall. "Don't move a muscle," he says as he begins kissing and touching, running his tongue over one set of lips and fingers over the other. She begins pulling tiny bits of air as his touch begins to build her.

The man who knows every inch of his woman gentles her to within a whisper of release. He turns her and raises her hands to chest level on the wall and lifts her hips back toward him. He enters her inch by inch, reaching his hands around to continue his touching. He lets her take control as she moves her hips back and forth, taking the length of him, then letting some go, then taking it again. His touch releases her. The tightening waves pull him to his edge and then over—she becomes gripped by one of **those** orgasms. Malcolm wraps his arms beneath their bump and lets her ride it. When she begins coming down, he pulls free and turns her to him. She begins to shake and smile and shake and giggle and shake and tease.

"Woman, that's enough."

She continues to tease. Her hands and fingers move across him, down the length of him, around the length of him.

Malcolm groans low and long, "Woman, let's take this to our bed."

Gretchen doesn't wait for the touching and the kissing and the mewing and the tiny pulls of air of their lovemaking. As soon as he is flat on his back, she straddles her man and takes him— all of him.

Malcolm tries to slow his woman's roll, but she is already way ahead of him. Her moans fill the space, her limbs begin to quiver, and her velvety space swells and tightens. Soft light illuminates her face. He enjoys her beauty and excites at the sight of her build and release. The man fills with an intensity of love for the woman who owns every part of him.

When he can, he lifts her from his shaft, lays her flat, and rises over her. He looks deeply into her cornflower blues, "Woman the way you undo me is near criminal."

Gretchen touches her man's face, "I think you mean, the way I **do** you is near criminal," she teases.

"That too," Malcolm laughs.

Not for self, but for others.

Election Day

Every room of the penthouse apartment at 275 Market Street is elbow to elbow with family, friends, and campaign workers—who are now family and friends. Gretchen is over the moon when Manuel Xavier and Fred Serpico step off the privacy elevator to join the celebration.

"We heard you were in town. I'm so glad you came!"

Fred receives his hug and kiss, then Manuel receives his. He wraps his arms around his friend, then eases her back to arm's length to take in the sight of her beautiful form. He places a hand to her bump and is rewarded with a kick.

"You are as beautiful as any expectant mother I've ever seen, Gretchen." He pulls her in again and hugs her tight, then laughs when he hears Malcolm's growl from behind. "Needn't worry, man. I have a thing for the other woman in your life," Manuel says as he makes a beeline for Mama Girl.

Malcolm calls after him, "Not sure I'm favoring that thing you have for my mother, Mr.

Xavier. I'm thinking about having you escorted to the borough line."

"After I make my moves, Mr. Mayor." Manuel comes to a sliding halt at his favorite girl.

"You lookin' for some love, boy?"

"Yes, ma'am," he wraps his arms tight.

"You still have a woman because I'm not the sharing kind? Tell me, how's relations with that woman of yours?"

"Muriel is fine." Manuel's smile is warm, but doesn't quite reach his eyes.

The astute woman notices and nudges, notices and judges, "You need to deal in whole truths, Manuel. Half-truths will leave your bed cold—even if there's a warm body in it."

Manuel nods and takes Mama Girl's hand.

She gives a gentle squeeze and changes subject. "And how is baby Charlotte?"

"Bringing me a kind of love I never imagined."

"The small ones don't have nothin' but love to bring, boy. Wait 'til she starts movin' and shakin'—that will be her announcement of who she is deep down. She'll go and dump it all at your feet. That's when the fun begins," a knowing Mama Girl laughs.

Shortly before 3 PM, The Kid and The Justice go from room to room turning on television sets. All screens are turned to a live shot of a bank of microphones set in front of the fountain at Forsyth Park in Savannah,

Georgia. Bertha King Price recognizes the fountain as the place that set in motion the events that brought them to where they all are today. She smiles at the full-circle being affectionately acknowledged by the only man she has ever loved. A low excitement begins to roll through the rooms pulling Bertha from her sentimental thoughts. She is joined by Granger and Faye and Gretchen and Malcolm who places his hand on his mother's shoulder. The family shares a hug before the announcement begins.

The Announcement

Senator Curtis Robert Morgan, holding the hand of his wife, Madison, steps to the microphones and simply says, "I would be honored to serve the people of this great Nation as president of the United States—if they will have me. I declare my candidacy and humbly request your vote on November 3, 2020. And to my son, Malcolm Price, congratulations on becoming Mayor of Lewisburg, Pennsylvania."

275 Market Street erupts in cheers. When the phone call from his father comes in, Malcolm asks for and is given complete silence. "Thank you, sir, and congratulations to you ……. Yes, sir, she is right here."

Malcolm hands the phone to Mama Girl.

Bertha King Price feels the stare of the entire room. "Curtis, congratulations. You will make a fine President .... Of course, I remember, Curtis. You said the foundation of your campaign would be, Non Sibi, Sed Aliis – not for self, but for others."

275 Market Street erupts into utter pandemonium.
Bertha King Price swells with pride and joy.

Diving deep innuendos.

It's Tuesday. Benton Brettenvue crawls from his personal torture chamber and makes his way to the windows across the room. He peeks out and surveys the back of his property, "So far, so good." He inches his way out of the den and across the hallway to his bedroom. He scans the front yard and the circular drive from a pair of massive windows. "It's about fucking time," he whoops as he sprints along the top floor of the house. He enters rooms along the way taking a peek here, a look there, careful to check the perimeter from different vantage points. He finds nothing and no one on his property. "I'm alone." He draws the first unencumbered breath he's had in days and exhales it on a huge sigh of relief.

The soon-to-be-man-on-the-run books it through the rest of the house, then into the attached garage. He gets into the shit box Toyota Tacoma the gardener uses, checks the back floor for the gear he put there, presses the garage door opener, pulls on a ballcap and a pair of sunglasses, and drives away.

Old Estate Road
Celia Brettenvue is perched on the living room couch waiting for her 8 PM check-in. She is

eager to end this day and begin the next. "Tomorrow, I see Dominique," her voice catches with ……. excitement? Something akin to butterflies flutter deep inside and her hands being to tremble. She gets lost in her attempt to remember the last time she saw her daughter—and not on some newsreel as being part of The Realm story, but in person. She just can't seem to remember. She is startled from her thoughts by a knock on the front door.

"Come in."

"Good evening, ma'am," Crew Cut #1 says.

"Good evening, Agent."

"A reminder, ma'am. Agents from the Philadelphia field office will be here tomorrow morning to accompany you and Attorney Mitchell to the penitentiary."

"Thank you."

"Are you ready to retire, ma'am?"

"Yes, Agent."

"Goodnight, then."

Philly

Fred Serpico and Manuel Xavier are back at Abigail Forrester's condo, rolling their sleeves. They're in for an all-nighter to make up for time lost at the celebration for Mayor Price. Detective Serpico is in the upstairs master bedroom processing some shit in front of some window.

Manuel is in the living room reviewing copious financial files and making a recording of his findings. "On the surface, Abigail Forrester supported herself nicely as a political consultant, but there are long periods of time when she wasn't pulling a paycheck, but was banking big bucks."

He clicks off the recorder, shuffles through some papers, then begins dictating and recording again, "There are W-2s filed with her yearly taxes that document who she was working for and her compensation for each quarter. There is nothing to indicate she owned her own company. Everything so far indicates she was hired into a management level position and put onto the payroll of a politician or political organization. Paystubs and bank deposits link up with the filed tax documents, however, there is a handwritten ledger that details another financial stream for Ms. Forrester. The ledger gives a picture of what Ms. Forrester did during intermittent periods of unemployment, at least it tracks where she was when she was doing whatever it was she was doing. I suspect the information in her home office will fill in the backstory of this ledger. From what I can piece together so far, the financial accounting matches trip itineraries with expense vouchers and receipts for travel throughout Pennsylvania. Within days of each return home there was a cash deposit of $25,000-$75,000 made into her bank account."

The investigator does the whole recorder-on-recorder-off-thing, then calls Leavy at RFI, "I just found a red flag in Abigail Forrester's financials dating back to 1999."

"That's when she interned for the Congressman," Leavy pushes in.

"And went to Georgetown."

"Looks like I'm going for a dive on you…for you…for you. Oh, for fuck's sake." There is dead air on the line. "Manuel, where'd you go?"

"Sorry, just got lost in a visual of you ….. never mind."

"Oh, for fuck's sake. Get your head…"

Manuel starts to laugh at her turn of phrase.

"Oh, for fuck's sake." Leavy hangs up.

Old Estate Road
Granger and Faye Mitchell return from the mayoral party a little after 10 PM. They check in with the Federal agents who inform them that Celia Brettenvue was lights out shortly after 8 PM.

"Just a reminder, Agents, Mrs. Brettenvue and I have a prisoner meeting at the penitentiary tomorrow."

"Yes, sir. Goodnight, sir."

The Compound

Leavy calls Manuel within minutes of his request, "There is no record of Abigail, or her parents, paying one red cent toward her studies at Georgetown. Additionally, there are no records of loans or grants being requested, offered, or disbursed from the University's financial aid office. Abigail submitted her application after deadline, attached a glowing recommendation from Turner Rodgers, who requested her admissions package be expedited through the process, and who was listed as the contact person on her financials. During the time of her attendance, tuition, fees and living expenses were close to thirty thousand per year—she spent three years at the University. If the Congressman paid for her education, he shelled out nearly $100,000."

"Good work, Leavy." Manuel is about to hang up when she asks, "Can I go diving on Turner Rodgers?"

"NO!"

"Not enjoying **that** visual, Manuel?" she laughs. "Goodnight, Manuel."

"Goodnight, Leavy."

It is many seconds before either of the two disconnects from the call.

A criminal event?

Celia Brettenvue does not answer the 8 AM knock on the Carriage House door. Federal agents enter the premises with guns drawn in search of their subject. It is a short search. They find their charge dead in her bed—the apparent victim of a homicide.

"Secure Granger and Faye Mitchell," #1 directs #2. As she sprints from the premises, she hears her partner say, "We have a problem, Director Remington. Celia Brettenvue is dead. It appears she was strangled. There is duct tape across her mouth, and it looks as though there is something stuffed inside."

Stacy Remington gives her order, "Do not call the local authorities. Guard the premises from outside the Carriage House. The only people allowed inside that building are Manuel Xavier and Fred Serpico. They are detectives with RFI. They will secure the scene and instruct you until I get there. Is that understood, Agent?"

"Yes, ma'am."

The Director calls Manuel Xavier, "You and Serpico need to be at Granger Mitchell's place in Philadelphia before I hang up from this call. Celia Brettenvue is dead. Her killing is identical to the one you are currently investigating. You and Fred are in charge of the scene until I get there. No one gets in but me."

I-76 W
Benton Brettenvue is a happy man. In the trunk of his newly boosted, cherry red Chevy Camaro are three duffle bags holding enough cash to last him a lifetime. "It won't be a lavish life, but it will be a life," he accepts. "All I need to do is get to Beaver Falls." The man howls in laughter at the name of his destination. "Beaver Falls. How fucking appropriate. All my beavers have fallen. One by fucking one the backstabbing bitches met their fate." Benton puts the Camaro in overdrive and races toward freedom. *Philadelphia Freedom*, he begins to sing.

Old Estate Road
Granger Mitchell places a call to Malcolm Price upon learning of Celia's demise. "Malcolm, do you have privacy at the moment?"

"Yes," he answers, already on alert.

The attorney pauses until he finds the right words, "I am not at liberty to explain the circumstances, but there has been a criminal event at the Carriage House. News will be breaking at some point today, and you will have a better understanding. I just wanted to let you know Faye and I are in fine health and our involvement in the event pertains to legal representation only. I'm sorry for the cloak and dagger nature of this call, but it cannot be helped at this time. Please make sure Gretchen doesn't become upset over this."

"I understand, Granger. If you need anything, please let me know," the mayor-elect disconnects from the call.

Granger places a call to LewPen and asks that inmate BOP-PA-555925 be informed her attorney is unable to attend their scheduled meeting. He asks the security officer to submit a visitation request on his behalf for the following Wednesday. When he disconnects, he concerns himself with Dominique's reaction to the news of her mother's death. His concern turns quickly to irritation. He fumes about the murdered woman on his estate. "Dammit all! I **needed** Celia if I am to help Dominique! Dammit all, Faye was in danger!" The man who is rarely pushed over the edge of anger, punches in a phone number. The call is answered before he has cooled down. "Stacy, it's Granger. What the hell happened?"

"I'm boarding a plane as we speak."

"What time should we expect you?"

"At your front door in two hours."

Chevy Chase
Boston, aka Paul Ferraro, aka contract killer to The Realm, calls his wife early afternoon, "Hey babe, sorry I didn't make it back before you headed out this morning. How are the troops?"

"The twins are missing you, maybe you could scale back on the trips," she says with a devilish laugh.

"I'll have to check with my boss, she's a slave driver. How about we do a mid-week pizza night for the kids and let them camp out with us?" The husband can feel his wife's smile over the phone. "I can tell you like that idea," he says playfully.

"Love it," Felicity says as she disconnects the call.

The killer-for-hire checks one of his offshore accounts to make sure his fee was deposited. Then he transfers the money out of the Cayman Islands and sends it around the globe.

275

After Malcolm gets his thoughts in order, he goes in search of his wife. He finds her perched on their conversation couch. He lifts her legs, sits near, and places them on his lap. He begins massaging her swollen feet, "How are you, Woman?"

"I'm tired, today. You know, Malcolm, 78 is due in two months."

He nods and smiles, "I'm aware."

"We need to think about a nursery." The mom-to-be grabs a baby magazine that's tucked next to her. "And apparently, there are a million things the smallest humans on the planet are in need of. I'm starting to panic, Malcolm. I have absolutely no idea about baby-raising. I think I might have held a baby once before, but I wouldn't swear to that fact in a court of law. What on earth makes us think I'm a good candidate for motherhood? And you, you're going to be too busy being Mr. Mayor to offer any real help. So it will be me and DelRae trying to figure this whole thing out, and we don't even have a nursery to put her in, and…"

Malcolm takes his woman's hand, "Come with me."

Gretchen accepts the hoist from the comforts of the couch and follows her man to the rarely used entertainment room.

"I talked with Stephanie Braun at Braun Architect and asked her to do a construction project," he begins.

Gretchen smiles.

"I'm having this room turned into a combo game and entertainment center. Stephanie says the current game room can be sectioned into a nice sized nursery with an attached playroom, and across from that there will be a large family room."

Gretchen's smile widens. "That sounds perfectly wonderful, Malcolm. I know just how I want to decorate the spaces. How soon will construction begin?"

"The game room will be stripped of memorabilia today with most of the stuff heading to the campaign space for storage. I'll go through the pieces, choose what I want to keep, and maybe auction some for charity. The construction crews will be in at 7 tomorrow morning to gut the entertainment room. Stephanie says everything will be done by Christmas."

Gretchen trudges her swollen feet toward her husband and pulls his face toward her for a kiss. "Well done, Mr. Mayor, you've made one citizen of Lewisburg very happy today. Come Friday, after the swearing in ceremony, you'll have to start chipping away at the other 6,200 residents of our fair borough."

Malcolm wraps his arms around his wife, "You and 78 will always come first." Their little girl responds with a happy little two-step that fills her parents with unbridled joy.

Malcolm leads Gretchen back to their conversation couch. After he settles her, he tells her about Granger's call—which sets her off on one of her word mashes.

"A criminal event? Daddy said those words, exactly? In my Carriage House? Well, technically it's Daddy's Carriage House, but it's been my home for the past two years, well up until I came here. And he said this criminal event will be on the news today? That is perplexing. I mean, it's probably not a burglary, that sort of thing doesn't warrant a breaking news event. And you said Daddy made it a point to tell you that he and Faye are, how did you put it…in fine health and that their involvement pertains to legal representation only. And he apologized for the cloak and dagger nature of his call, and that this situation needn't worry me. Well, perhaps it needn't worry me, but it does worry me."

Malcolm patiently waits until his woman's word mashing winds down, "Gretchen, are you finished?"

"For now."

"I think you missed the part where your father didn't want you to become upset over this. Can you calm down until we know what's happening?"

Gretchen nods.

"Good, I'll be in the office if you need me." Malcolm kisses the top of her head and runs his fingers through her cropped hair, "I love this, Charlize."

Gretchen's smile runs ear to ear. She picks up a decorating magazine, turns on MSNBC, and waits for breaking news.

Stating the obvious.

FICA Director Remington has the two Federal agents who were on duty the night before accompany her inside the Carriage House. Fred and Manuel have already performed a walk-through of the premises and determined there was a colossal fuck up with the security detail.

"Explain yourselves, Agents."

Crew Cut #1 explains, "We performed the 8 PM security check. It was lights out for Mrs. Brettenvue immediately after that. I made the call to skip the next two checks."

"Explain."

"We were sitting in a vehicle parked no more than twenty-feet from the premises with sight on both doors."

Stacy takes a step away from the agents, "Detectives Serpico and Xavier, please confiscate the agents' firearms and badges."

Fred and Manuel do as they are asked.

"Manuel, please cuff the agents together. Escort them to their vehicle and lock them inside. Stay with them until further notice." The FICA Director makes a call to FBI Director, Shelby Webber. "Ma'am, I'm at the murder scene of Celia Brettenvue. I have released two agents from service."

"Explain."

"The agents in discussion performed their last security check at 8 PM on a 4-hour cycle. The victim was found deceased at 8 AM having had no security check for a 12-hour period. Permission to hold them at the Philadelphia field office for questioning?"

"Detain them on-site. I'll have agents bring them in. Keep me informed, Director Remington."

"Of course, ma'am."

Stacy turns her attention to Fred, "I'd like your input, Detective."

"Stating the obvious, ma'am, it's way too coincidental that the agents didn't do their mandated checks, Celia was left alone for twelve hours, a killer showed up during that time frame and had uninterrupted access to the star witness in your Tango investigation."

Stacy thumps across the room, "Sometimes the obvious needs to be stated, Detective, no matter how much it is going to piss me off. Take me to the victim."

275

Gretchen shouts for Malcom just before 5 PM. "Shhhhh," she points to the television as he makes a running entrance. A news anchor announces the breaking news…

"Celia Brettenvue, mother of Dominique Brettenvue, was found murdered in the Carriage House on the Philadelphia estate of famed attorney, Granger Mitchell. According to sources, Celia Brettenvue was under FBI protective custody at the Mitchell estate. She was set to provide Federal authorities information on a clandestine operation known as Tango. Sources close to the investigation link Tango to the disbanded criminal organization known as The Realm. Dominique Brettenvue, who is currently serving a life-sentence at the U.S. Penitentiary in Lewisburg, and Peruvian crime lord, Antonio Alvarez, currently awaiting trial at the ADX Supermax Penitentiary in Florence, Colorado, have ties to The Realm and to Tango."

Gretchen is about to begin one of her word mashes when she receives a call from her father.

"Gretchen."

"Daddy, I just heard. You and Faye are fine, right? I mean there was a killer on your property last night. Oh, Daddy, poor Celia, I mean I was not a fan of the woman, but that doesn't matter now, does it? How did she die, only if it wasn't gruesome, I don't want 78 hearing terrible things, but of course it must have been gruesome and—"

"Gretchen, please take a breath," Granger interrupts, "it's probably best for me to speak with Malcolm. Is he nearby?"

Gretchen hands her husband the phone, "The elitist sexist pig wants to talk with you."

Malcolm laughs and takes the phone, "Yes, sir, I'll tell Gretchen you heard her comment."

Gretchen groans and pushes down into the couch, hoping it will swallow her whole.

Old Estate Road

Stacy Remington thumps across the room after transferring custody of two agents. She listens to the third breaking news report in an hour. This time, more detailed information about Tango, The Realm, and a mysterious figure known only as The Body, is being bandied about—these names should not be bandied about. She points to a coffee table, "Manuel, take a picture of the table."

He shoots Fred a look, then takes several pictures of said table from several angles.

"Thank you. Now please step away." The extremely pissed-off woman places a foot onto the coffee table, gives it a mighty push, flipping it ass end to. Her angry grunt reverberates throughout the space. She moves toward the door and calls over her shoulder, "Manuel, please return the coffee table to its original position. I'll be outside for a few minutes." She places another phone call to FBI Director Webber. There is no pause on Webber's end.

"What the hell happened? Who the hell leaked Tango? And why is the press talking about The Body and The Realm?"

"At this time, ma'am, I have no idea how the media learned about any of this. I feel confident it did not come from this end."

"Director Remington, there is a dead witness who has been linked to an operation that is linked to The Realm an organization we thought was decimated. Find out who knows about Tango."

Stacy disconnects from the very heated Shelby Webber and heads back inside. "Manuel, I want you to list everyone involved with The Realm who knows about Tango. I want to do a mental check against your list."

"The imprisoned Realm leaders: Antonio Alvarez of Peru, Binto Dube of Africa, Castro López of Argentina, Julio Romero of Chile, Raphael Ruiz of Brazil, Stiles Sigüenza of Guatemala, Miguel Sosa of Columbia, former FICA Director, Roland Gaffney, former FICA Agent, Dan Shea, and imprisoned Realm associate, Dominique Brettenvue. In addition to those individuals, we believe Benton and Celia Brettenvue knew about Tango, and since Abigail Forrester was Benton's mistress and spent time in the company of Antonio Alvarez, she probably knew, as well."

Stacy analyzes and opines, "As soon as Tango came onto our radar, Benton Brettenvue was on it, too. We've been trying to bring him in for questioning, but he's in the wind. Mr. Brettenvue currently holds the distinction of being the only person linked to Tango who isn't in prison, in a morgue, or heading to one. Evidence suggests he has a great deal to lose if we uncover the scope of Tango."

Fred pushes in. "Stating the obvious, ma'am, Benton Brettenvue had a motive for the Abigail Forrester and Celia Brettenvue murders."

"Stating the obvious is becoming a thing, Detective Serpico," the Director quips.

"Yes, ma'am."

Manuel pushes in, "Director, I think we should consider the possibility that Senator Turner Rodgers knows about Tango, The Realm, and The Body."

She says nothing. She shows nothing. She simply thumps from the Carriage House.

Octopus

When she returns from Philadelphia, Stacy goes directly to her home office. She locks herself behind closed doors and gets to work. Several hours later she is ready to review her work. On her third pass through, something intriguing jumps out at her…

Organizational Structure:
The Body
8 ancillary leaders: 6 from South America, 1 from Africa, 1 from the U.S.

Arrests:
Antonio Alvarez: Peru
Binto Dube: Africa
Roland Gaffney: United States
Castro López: Argentina
Julio Romero: Chile
Raphael Ruiz: Brazil
Stiles Sigüenza: Guatemala
Miguel Sosa: Columbia
* Dominique Brettenvue: United States
           (potential replacement leader)
* Dan Shea: United States (ancillary member)

She talks it through, "We arrested 8 leaders. What remained after the 8 leaders were arrested? The Body? The original structure was The Body and 8 leaders. What has a body and eight appendages. A spider. An octopus. The first operational goal of The Realm was to acquire cyber huntresses. They dive deep, like an octopus. The organizational structure might be an octopus."

She adds the word **octopus** to her organizational structure, prints two copies of the summary, puts one into an envelope addressed to Manuel Xavier and the other into an envelope addressed to Granger Mitchell.

Mayor

Malcolm Price is sworn in as Mayor of Lewisburg during a noontime ceremony. His wife is standing by his side. Watching from the front row are Bertha King Price, Senator and Mrs. Curtis Morgan, Granger and Faye Mitchell, The Kid and The Justice. The happy revelers are enjoying one another's company back at 275 Market Street when the ceremony is interrupted with MSNBC breaking news…

"Dominique Brettenvue, female leader of the disbanded criminal organization, The Realm, was found murdered in her cell at the U.S. Penitentiary at Lewisburg, earlier today..."

Granger Mitchell touches his breast pocket, feels the picture of Charlotte that rests there, then slams his hand on the table.

"Goddammit to Hell!"

The End

More to come …

Please enjoy the teaser for my next book in the series, *Tango…*

TANGO

THE RANGER

--- PULLING THREADS ---

Book Eleven

SHERYLL O'BRIEN

Dead Women Don't Talk

Abigail

He straddled her chest locking her arms beneath his knees and silencing her with a hand to her mouth. He put a loaded gun to her head, "If you make a sound, I will kill you. Do you understand?"

She nodded.

"I came to deliver a message. You need to listen to everything I have to say. I am going to gag you and tape your mouth shut. I will not hurt you if you cooperate. Do you understand?"

She nodded—opened her mouth—moaned pitifully.

He put a pair of silk panties in—taped her mouth shut—exhaled fully.

"Open your eyes, Abigail. Very good. Turner Rodgers does not want you in DC. He is taking back his block. Do you understand?"

She nodded.

"The Realm wants you dead."

Celia

He straddled her chest locking her arms beneath his knees and silencing her with a hand to her mouth. He put a loaded gun to her head.

"If you make a sound, I will kill you. Do you understand?"

She nodded.

"I came to deliver a message. You need to listen to everything I have to say. I am going to gag you and tape your mouth shut. I will not hurt you if you cooperate. Do you understand?"

She nodded—opened her mouth— whimpered pitifully.

He put a pair of silk panties in—taped her mouth shut—exhaled fully.

"Open your eyes, Celia. Very good. The Realm does not want you talking to the Feds about Tango. Do you understand?"

She nodded.

"The Realm wants you dead."

Dominique

He handed off a vial of poison. This is for prisoner BOP-PA-555925. From outside LewPen he sent the message, "The Realm wants you dead."

ABOUT THE AUTHOR

She is not dead.

Sheryll O'Brien crafts characters without constraints. She tells them who they are, then let's them show her better versions of themselves. She gives them life and they live it beyond her wildest dreams.

Sheryll is a lifelong resident of Worcester, Massachusetts, where she is wife to the most supportive husband ever, and mother of two adult daughters, one who refuses to leave her home and the other who refuses to tell her where she lives. Of most significance, she is MammyGrams to the sweetest six-year-old, Hadley.

Sheryll worked several years in the fundraising community of Worcester County, writing grants for non-profit organizations. She began writing for her own pleasure after surviving brain surgery and breast cancer. Happily, for her fanbase of family and friends-—she is not dead.

If you have enjoyed reading my book, I would very much appreciate you taking a few minutes to write a review and post that review on amazon.com and goodreads.com.

The opinion of readers can help prospective readers make a purchasing decision.

To learn more, please visit my website, www.pullingthreadsnovella.com subscribe to my blog for updates on future projects.

I would absolutely love to hear from my readers, you can email me at,

pullingthreadsnovella@gmail.com

www.ingramcontent.com/pod-product-compliance
Lightning Source LLC
Chambersburg PA
CBHW070824180626
46818CB00001B/391